A Twisted Journey

and

OTHER SHORT ADVENTURES

A Twisted Journey

and

OTHER SHORT ADVENTURES

ROBERT D. ANDREWS

Order this book online at www.trafford.com
or email orders@trafford.com

Most Trafford titles are also available at major online book retailers.

Printed in the United States of America.

ISBN: 978-1-4669-1581-7 (sc)
ISBN: 978-1-4669-1580-0 (e)

Trafford rev. 05/29/2012

Trafford PUBLISHING® www.trafford.com

North America & international
toll-free: 1 888 232 4444 (USA & Canada)
phone: 250 383 6864 ♦ fax: 812 355 4082

CONTENTS

Part II
Short Adventures

Chapter 1

Nigel was taking his usual moonlight swim at the beach in front of his house. It had been a fruitful day! He had made two major sales and was celebrating in his usual way.

As he lay face down, blowing bubbles, bouncing with the rhythm of the water, a shadowy figure, seeming to come from nowhere, pushed forcefully on Nigel's head and neck, banging his head on the rocks under him. There was not even a brief struggle and bubbles stopped coming through the water. Only the foam of the ocean lazily floating back and forth in the moonlight was visible.

When the tenseness in Nigel's body turned to a slumped relaxedness, the shadowy figure let go of the body, moved back to the shore and slipped into the shadows among the dark shrubs.

Tammy was in the house, unaware of the events outside. She looked again at the invitation and reached for the glass containing the scotch. Her movement was erratic, and she knocked the glass on the floor-that damn green and gray tile floor-ice cubes, glass and fluid flowing across the floor reminding her of the tide flowing in, carrying unwanted debris. The broken glass was scattered across the floor, some pieces pushing up against the slider door that faced the ocean.

As Tammy mumbled to herself, she heard a noise at the side door. "Nigel?" she called out hesitantly. Nigel always used the back entrance through the slider when he took his swim. Tammy listened for a response, but there was none. Then she heard the doorknob rattle. Her chest tightened. She tried to clear the alcohol haze by shaking her head.

Her first impulse was to run out the back where she could find Nigel, but the entire entranceway was strewn with glass. She looked at her feet, realizing she was ready for bed. She wore a light, transparent robe covering her dainty blue bikini panties covered with pink flowers, and nothing else. She was barefoot.

She shook her head again, trying to clear her mind.

She heard another noise coming from the side door, a slight banging noise. Tammy ran up the open stairway to her bedroom. She closed the door quietly and locked it. She avoided turning on the light. The moonlight streamed through the window, with more than enough light for her to find the phone. Tammy felt a strange feeling in her stomach when she picked up the phone and found no dial tone. The phone was dead.

She looked around the room. A soft teddy bear and piles of fluffy pillows would not be very helpful weapons.

She heard a "bump" noise downstairs, like someone moving furniture. Her senses were alert. Her breath was rapid. "Don't panic!" she whispered to herself.

She stuffed some of the pillows under the down-turned cover of the bed and put the bear on the pillow. She then pulled the blanket up so it just covered the stuffed animal. In the moonlight, it appeared as if someone was in the bed. She hoped the diversion would buy her precious time. The bathroom door had an old-fashioned key. She took out the key and put it in the bedroom side of the lock. She hesitated a moment, reached in the bathroom, grabbing a dark gray shower cap, leaving two others, one with bright yellow and red circles and the other with an array of brightly colored stars.

She closed and locked the bathroom door, took the key out of the lock and slide it under the bed. She moved toward the slider door and took the one inch dowel stick they used to block the slider door to the porch, went to the porch and closed the slider. She placed the stick on the outside so the door would not open.

As she was bending over, the bedroom door flew open, light slicing through the door. She stayed crouched by the door as the shadowy figure slowly came into the bedroom. As he turned to the left toward the bed, the light revealed a face of a thirty-fiveish year old man with dark curly hair and a fuzzy beard and mustache. He raised his arm and the light reflected on the blade of the large kitchen knife in his hand.

He yelled as he ran toward the bed. As he moved, Tammy ran down the stairs and toward the left side of the beach where there was some shrubs. Tammy realized the shrubs would not hide her and she ran toward the water.

She could hear the prowler banging on the door. She couldn't tell if it was the bathroom door or the porch slider, praying it was the bathroom door. He might see her if it was the porch door.

She remembered the shower cap in her hand and pulled it over her bright yellow hair, then tucked the long locks under the cap so they would not show. The tide was coming in and the swells were getting larger. Tammy submerged herself so nothing of her was visible except the part of her face she needed to breathe.

It became very quiet except for the breaking of the waves. Tammy let her body float back and forth with the water until it brought her too close to the shore. When it did, she would push herself back into deeper water where the swells had not yet broken into waves.

A few clouds dimmed the intense brightness of the moon. It was then Tammy saw him. He came back out of the house through the side door on the first floor. He moved toward the bushes, then toward the edge of the water. He walked slowly along the edge of the shore. As he neared where she was, Tammy let herself sink, and grabbed two rounded rocks about the size of oranges for weapons. She stayed down as long as she could, then slowly came up and took a breath. The shadowy figure was further down the beach. He turned, scanning the water, and Tammy sunk again under the water.

When she came up for the next breath, the clouds were covering the moon. She could not see him, but went under the water again, pushing herself into the water a little deeper. She could feel the tide pushing her to her right, the same direction the man was going. She knew it was useless to fight the tide, so she let it drift her farther and farther down the beach away from the house.

It had been dark about ten minutes when the moon came out again, lighting up everything. Tammy, coming up for air, looked around quickly, alert for any movement on the beach. She saw nothing, but knew he might be hiding in the shadows almost anywhere, waiting for her to make her move. The stones grew difficult to hold. She let one go, switching the other from one tired hand to the other.

It seemed like hours when Tammy finally saw a house lit up, just a little farther down the beach. It was late in the season, and a weekday. Many of the houses were empty. As she floated in front of the house, she could see a middle-aged couple through the window. Both were reading.

Tammy was hesitant about coming out of the water, but she was tired and cold. She let a wave carry her nearer the shore. When in about eight inches of water, she gripped her rock, got up and ran toward the house. She ran up the stairs and pounded on the glass slider door facing the beach, startling the occupants. They both came to the door and slid it opened.

"Please! You must help me! A man is trying to kill me!"

The woman looked at Tammy, then, after a slight hesitation, moved aside. "Must have been one hell of a party!" she said dryly. Tammy was not sure what she meant until she unconsciously pulled the cap off her head and let her blond hair cascaded across her shoulders. When she saw the half smile on the man's appreciative face, she became aware of her wet and revealing outfit.

"Come with me, honey," said the woman. "Let's get you a robe. And you, Edward, put your eyes on the phone and call the police. Then get your gun, just in case the creep is still around!"

Chapter 11

Tammy was starting to feel 'sick' again—that combination of fear and paranoia. She hadn't had an attack for two months.

"I really am feeling better," she insisted, when she talked to Bill Buxton and Maxwell Pennington, her business partners. Bill wasn't convinced. He was the one who was constantly at her side since the incident. He was the one who talked to the police after her fifth false accusation of another man with a beard. Max had kept more of a distance but was the one who had arranged for the psychiatrist.

It was now six months since the home invasion and death of her husband, Nigel Burroughs. She was there at the time of the break-in and had escaped from the second floor of her summer home at the beach. She hid in the waves and watched the man in the house—a man with a beard—a man hunting her. The moon had come in and out as she drifted with the current, past several empty houses, before she came before a house with lights. It was only then she left the water, armed with a rock, and ran to the house. It was shortly after the police found the body of her husband on the beach among a cove of rocks with his head crushed.

She really had been feeling better. The medication took a few weeks and some adjustments before it started helping, but she was stabilized now, and wanted the comfort and structure of the art gallery back in her life.

Her partners were concerned about her intense and unusual reaction when she saw the work of Andrew Parks. Max was especially proud of the contract he had negotiated with him. Max was the business genius of the organization. He was boyishly excited to tell Tammy about the details. He saw her as his financial protégée and knew she would recognize the fine points of the contract. He didn't get a chance to share. Tammy had reacted to Andrew's paintings with an intense hate and strong reaction he had never seen from her, and was puzzled. Andrew was the new darling of the art world. To get a commitment from him was a coup. To finalize the financial agreement they did was even more of an accomplishment. Later, she calmed. She acknowledged Max's good contracting work and he was pleased. Bill remained perplexed. His public relations sensitivity knew something wasn't balanced and was concerned about her response to a popular artist, especially since it was part of their role to make him famous—and everybody a little richer.

Tonight was the night of their introduction of Andrew as their client. It would be a posh party, including the members of their advisory board and special patrons. She stopped at the corner of the building and took some deep breaths. "Good thoughts. I need good memories," she murmured, and then thought of Nigel. They had met at a party like this. Nigel was attractive, single, and seemed enamored by her. She had worked at The Gallery for two years after graduating from art school, but it wasn't until the party that she met him. He saw her as his princess, and after a whirlwind romance laced with exotic trips and tons of flowers, they were married. There was something in his spontaneity that appealed to her artistic nature, and his seemingly unlimited financial resources allowed him to behave like a playful young boy.

Thoughts of an alive, nurturing Nigel comforted her. She thought of Bill Buxton, who was there when she needed him, always seeming to know what to say and what to do. She took another deep breath, and walked in the entrance to The Gallery complex. Susan Stone, the administrator, sat at a table ready to greet people and give directions.

"Oh, Tammy, how good to have you back! We've all missed you." Susan gave Tammy a cautious hug. "You look wonderful!" She took Tammy's hands and stepped back, admiring her. "Oh, a heads-up—Alice Gibson, our special patron, is here!" Tammy smiled. "Thanks for the warning," she laughed. Both the women smiled, and then Tammy moved toward a rest room. "Last minute check—great to be to be back," and waved at Susan.

In the rest room, Tammy examined herself. She did look good. She was surprised that the churning feelings inside her didn't seem to show. Her conservative business suit fit perfectly, dark blue against a white high-neck blouse. A cameo graced her throat and not one blond hair was out of place. As she checked her nails next to her lip coloring, she smiled as she saw her wedding ring, still on her finger and thought "I'm not alone."

Chapter III

*T*ammy headed toward The Gallery where voices, laughter, and clinks of glasses echoed. As she got closer, her sensory system seemed to get more alert, hearing and seeing things she might have missed at a different time or place. She could feel her energy flow in her body, as if erasing the fear and paranoia that had been growing again and had been her companion for four of the six past months. She took a deep breath and whispered "yes" to herself.

At the edge of the group, she greeted people she knew, looking for Bill or Max. "Hello." The voice at her elbow surprised her and she felt herself jump. "Dad!" She was genuinely surprised. She knew he disliked these affairs and said he felt out of place with all the snobs. "I didn't expect to see you here. What a delight." She *was* glad to see him. He provided company and presence in her home after the event until a month ago, when Tammy suggested that he return to his own house. She knew he missed hanging out with his detective friends and retired police buddies and had grown very bored.

"Ah, I just wanted to be here for my Sweetie's coming-out party." He smiled warmly, then, in a half whisper, asked "You all right?"

She nodded, "Thanks for asking."

He glanced at the paintings. "I didn't know you were painting again."

"I'm not. Why did you think that?"

"Aren't these your paintings?" He swept his hand around the room.

"No, of course not! These are by Andrew Parks and I don't like them." she hissed.

"Whoa! Sorry! They look like the kind of thing you used to paint."

She caught her anger in time, she thought, and asked "Have you seen Bill or Max?"

"Not yet. It was Bill who suggested I come and he said he'd be here."

"Good. And thanks for coming. I'm going to mingle now."

She saw Bill and his wife Janet talking to another couple. Bill greeted her enthusiastically. He pulled her into the conversation after the usual greetings. Tammy could feel Janet examining her as if looking for a flaw. "She'll find none," Tammy thought. "I'm perfect tonight." Then she realized the strength of energy flowing through her. "If anyone tries anything with me, tries to harm me, I'll rip them apart with my bare hands!" Tammy was surprised at the tension and aggressiveness of her thoughts. She smiled at Janet when Janet glanced at her again.

Janet leaned over and said "What an ordeal you've been through. I don't know how I could have survived. And you! You look so—so beautiful! I admire you so!" She reached up and touched Tammy's cheek as gently as a feather, as she looked into her eyes and returned Tammy's smile.

Bill broke in. "I'm going to steal Tammy away for a moment. I want her to meet our guest of honor." He took Tammy's elbow and pointed her to the other side of the room. "What do you think of the gathering?" he asked.

"Well, it looks like you've got all the right people." She looked at him as he stopped for a moment. "How are you feeling? Are you OK?" His face was serious, the usual smile gone.

"I'm fine, great in fact—my old self!" "Am I over assuring him?" she wondered.

"We've been through some tough times, and I need to warn you before you meet Andrew." He hesitated. "Andrew has a beard. If it's going to throw you into a tizzy, avoid meeting him tonight. We can't afford a scene like we had a few months ago with the beard thing. It's your call."

Tammy was a little taken back. In her anger and resistance to Andrew's work, she had somehow missed the fact he wore a beard. She also knew in her former emotional state, she missed a lot of things, with every day being so heavy that just getting out of bed was an accomplishment.

Her mind whirled. There was a part of her that knew her resistance was well past the point of importance and there was business to be conducted. She also knew she had not seen anyone with a beard in the past few months. She also felt strong, yet she knew Bill's reservations were appropriate, based on her own behavior. Not once but five times she had reacted, sure it was the intruder, only to be wrong and needing sedation to be calmed.

"Have you had your meds?" Bill asked, kindly, yet firmly.

"Yes." She took a deep breath. "Let's do it. I feel good and knowing what to expect is helpful."

Bill paused and looked her in the eyes, as if searching for something. He sighed and said "OK, let's go."

A crowd of people surrounded Andrew Parks. Enthusiasm was high. Tammy knew this was a good sign, from a business point of view. For a moment, she wondered why her negative reaction to his paintings had been so strong. The crowd parted to let Bill and Tammy through. When Tammy saw him, prepared or not, she was startled. It was him! It was the man! The pursuer! The stalker! The murderer!

She swallowed the scream. She heard murmurs from Bill, and Andrew extended his hand toward her. She felt the automatic smile on her face. She reached forward and shook his hand. As her hand touched his, it felt as if a lightning bolt went through her body. It seemed as if Andrew had X-ray eyes and could see the hate within her very essence. She didn't see his smile. She didn't hear his greeting. She could only see black eyes and hear a voice whisper, "It's him, it's him. He's the one!"

She felt herself nod, a professional gesture to match the professional smile. She turned to Bill and asked, "Have you seen my father? Would you take me to him?" Bill understood she wanted to exit and led her away as the crowd enveloped Andrew.

Bill looked at Tammy and said, "That went smoothly! You did well, Tammy! I feel relieved. I guess you are better. Congratulations!" Bill was grinning ear to ear. Tammy remembered her visit to the rest room, looking in the mirror and seeing no external signs of her emotional state. She felt a wreck. Bill saw a composed, confident woman.

On the way across the room, Max appeared, grinning like a Cheshire cat. "I've got good news. Alice Gibson wants to see you, Tammy. She wants you to convince Andrew to make a special painting for her. You've worked with her before. She wants it to be you to assist with her request. If you're successful, she'll be very happy." Tammy looked at Max. She could see the dollar signs in his eyes and by the measure of his grin, a lot of money would be involved.

Bill offered, "She just met Andrew. It went well. I think Andrew's attracted to her."

"Good! Let's go find Alice." said Max.

Tammy said "NO!" then hesitated. Her mind was in rapid motion, clicking the conversation together. "No," she repeated more softly. "The timing is off."

"She's anxious to get a commitment tonight." Max's eyebrows were raised.

"Yes, of course, tonight, just a little later. Let him suck up the attention first, and then flatter him with the request. Timing! Isn't that what you taught me, Max?"

Bill was smiling. Her comment reassured him. He knew she was good at these things.

Tammy knew she needed time to compose herself. At this moment, she would be useless to Alice Gibson and didn't know how she would react to another encounter with Andrew if she were in this state of emotional turmoil. "Let's give it about an hour," she said with authority. Both men looked at their watches and nodded.

It was about an hour later when Max steered Alice Gibson toward Tammy. "Oh, it's so nice to have you back!" squealed Alice when she saw Tammy. "They're nice," nodding toward Max, "but you understand me. Oh, I'm so excited. Max told me to wait to see Andrew until you could go with me."

Tammy, warm on the outside, was now cold and steely on the inside, allowing her business persona to fill her body. She had taken an additional medication that was not on her approved list and it was effective, changing her ego state and numbing feelings, not only of fear, but of compassion.

Tammy listened closely to what Alice wanted, a picture of the Ascension of Mary in a modern painting. Tammy was aware that none of Andrew's painting had a religious theme, and she was aware she knew almost nothing about him. She usually did extensive research about an artist, knowing the quirks, styles, likes and dislikes before a venture such as this, but knew she would have to wing this one. Bill was talking with Andrew when the three of them joined the group. After the last couple left, the five stood together.

It was as if Tammy had a personality change. She now looked at Andrew and saw a young, handsome artist, full of confidence about his art, yet vulnerable to persuasion through flattery. She knew from Max that he was independently wealthy, as was Alice Gibson. "What a pair," she thought.

She suggested they retire to a small meeting room, explaining that we had a request of him.

"Yes, Bill told me you had a request that would be a pleasant surprise for me, but he wouldn't tell me what it was." Andrew was grinning and looking at Tammy. What she saw was different than only the hour before when she perceived this man as a monster. Now he seemed like an adolescent young man looking at a woman for the first time in his life. She was back in control. No fear. Icy determination. Bill excused himself and the four went to the conference room.

Andrew sat on the edge of the chair, excited to find out what they wanted. He looked so boyish and innocent that it almost made her smile, especially when she thought of the image she saw earlier. Tammy sat across from Andrew. Alice sat on one side, Max on the other. Tammy's voice was both seductive and business-like at the same time. As she spoke, she constantly looked in his eyes. His eyes never wandered away from her, and for him it seemed as if only two people were in the room. She mesmerized him, and when she got to the request, he had to ask her to repeat it. He was listening to her voice as he listened to music, unaware of the words. As she repeated the request, his focus came back into the room, hearing "Ascension of Mary."

His quick wit had him turn toward Alice, and asked her to explain what she wanted in her own words. Alice looked at Tammy and smiled, then at Andrew. "I just love your work. All my life I wanted my own picture of the Ascension of Mary in a modern style. Everything I've seen is so—so stuffy."

Andrew grinned. "I don't do religious pictures. I think they're too stuffy, too." They both laughed. He continued. "How old is the Mary you see in your mind?"

"I—I don't know, I never thought about it."

"Well, do you want a Mary, the Mother of a full grown man, or a young Mary? We can perform magic with art." His smile was engaging to Alice.

"Well, if I'm honest with myself, she's young, and beautiful, and pure looking in my mind's eye. That's part of the miracle I see."

"Yes, yes—this could be fun. I am sure that we could come up with a financial agreement that Max will negotiate, but I have only one request." He bent over and took her hand. "I will need a model. I will want some pictures of you at the age you want Mary. You will be my model. Would you be willing to provide me with pictures of yourself?"

Alice stammered in disbelief. "Oh—oh yes,—oh—of course." She was breathing hard.

Both Tammy and Max were smiling. Max thought, "What a pro! He's really good. Wow, is he smooth!"

Tammy excused herself when they started to negotiate money. This was Max's territory.

She felt euphoric and her inner ice started to thaw. She walked down the hall and saw a flashing light. She moved toward the light, but it seemed to move farther away from her. Then she realized the light she was seeing was a result of the medication. It was still working and changing her perceptions. Her body started to get warm all over. The icy feeling was replaced by the heat from a furnace. She moved quickly into an unoccupied office. She felt physically hot and could feel beads of sweat on her brow. Her body was sexually tense. She shook her head. In the corner, two figures appeared, Andrew Parks and a young version of Alice Gibson. They both looked at her as Alice lifted her leg and put it over Andrew's hip. As Andrew rubbed his hands over Alice, Tammy could feel hands over her.

"Damn, I'm hallucinating!" She left the office and looked for her father. "I was just about to leave," he said as she came close. "Hey, you look funny. You OK?"

"Dad, take me home. I'm done here. Take me home and stay with me tonight. I don't trust myself."

Charles Anderson's face got stony. He had heard phrases like that from his wife before she committed suicide. He hurried Tammy out of the building toward his car.

Chapter IV

Leonard Small had picked up Andrew at The Gallery. Leonard was an engineer who served as Andrew's man Friday and was a trusted friend. Andrew was usually shy around women, but would come to life when art was the subject. "So, how did it go?" asked Leonard.

"What a party! I made a good decision signing with them. Lots of great contacts, and guess what! I got a commission—to paint a picture for an obscene amount of money."

Leonard smiled. He knew Andrew didn't need any money and knew he was high on something else.

"So, what else?"

"I met a princess! Bright and beautiful—I think I'm in love."

"Does she know you're rich?"

"I don't know and I don't care. She's into art."

Leonard shook his head and smiled. "Good thing he's going to Europe for awhile," he thought.

Max called Tammy the next afternoon. "I wanted to share the results of your efforts with Alice and Andrew." He described the base of the negotiations and the result for The Gallery and Andrew. Tammy was still groggy, but she was stunned by what Max told her. "Wow, you're good!" she said.

"We're all good! Everybody's happy. I have an idea. How about meeting me at my office Monday morning? I've only had my picture to talk to since you've been gone. I miss our chats."

"Monday is fine. Is about 10 all right? I'm going to spend the rest of the week with my dad. Don't want to do too much too soon."

"Hell, you did more than a month's work last night. Glad to have you back. See you Monday."

Chapter V

Max was playing with charts of numbers and graphs when Tammy entered his office. She felt comfortable in this environment. The multi-patterned Oriental rug and ornately carved desk did not appeal to her taste, but Max loved the décor. It was their many discussions here that created the safe feelings she had in this room. A large framed picture of Max's mentor, Peter Whitman, was on his right, placed so he could swirl his chair to look at it.

While in high school, Max attended a lecture on business and profit by Peter Whitman, a well-known entrepreneur and investment specialist. Peter was impressed with the quality of Max's questions, especially compared to those by people many years his senior. After the lecture, Max stayed and talked more with Peter Whitman. Peter invited Max to lunch. That developed into regularly scheduled meetings, where both men enjoyed long discussions.

Peter funded much of Max's college education at Wharton, where Peter was a trustee. Their discussion continued during and beyond college. For Max, Peter was a financial guru. His Socratic method of teaching was a pleasant encounter for both of them. It had been Peter's suggestion that Max get involved in The Gallery, the most prestigious in the area.

Peter had died just before Tammy started working for The Gallery. She had outstanding references from her art school and became a successful employee, "adding value," Max said. He knew art from a technical and business angle, and she seemed to understand it from a more humanistic and feeling perspective. She was aware that she needed to know more about the financial end of the business, and Max thrived and enjoyed her questions. She helped fill a hole for Max, who now moved from student to mentor. He met with her two times a week in a mini, informal financial seminar, and was continuously impressed with her ability to stay interested and absorb the material he shared, reading everything he suggested.

After Tammy married Nigel Burroughs, Nigel began to understand how much she loved art and knew about finances. He became aware that she wanted to work, not stay at home, as he first expected. He encouraged her to buy a share in The Gallery. He told her to talk with Max to introduce the idea. If something could be done, he would negotiate a price with Max and Bill.

Max expressed interest. He had a lead on buildings in a transition neighborhood in Quebec that was quickly turning into an artist community with a group raising money to buy their own buildings. He felt if he could beat them out, they would be able to sell the buildings at a good profit. Then once the community had become established, start another gallery there, or do both.

He also had ideas about expanding and modernizing the current gallery, all with his eye on the bottom line. Max convinced Bill of the wisdom of his plans, and agreed to talk with Nigel. Max was very pleased with the outcome and a share in the partnership was made in Tammy's name.

"I only want owners in the family, not workers," Nigel confided to her one day after too much gin.

Max continued to meet with Tammy, discussing financial decisions he had to make, and ideas he wanted to test out. They became professional friends, each finding a sounding board for their ideas.

During Tammy's absence, he talked to Peter Whitman's picture, an old habit, and kidded with Tammy that it wasn't nearly as satisfying talking to the picture as it was talking with her.

"So, what's up?" she asked. Her head had cleared over the weekend and she felt comfortable sitting in her favorite chair.

"Well, first and foremost, I want you to get to know Andrew Parks inside out. I hear he plans to go to Europe soon. I'm wondering if we could get him to stay longer, or at least get an agreement where we would handle everything he does. We might even be able to get a Power of Attorney to enact all business for him if he's gone, rather than trying to track him down wherever he may go. It would be great if he also sent us new paintings. He has a reputation for disappearing when he's painting and he doesn't respond to much of anything during these periods."

"A Power of Attorney to do his business is pretty heavy duty. I don't know why he would do that." responded Tammy.

"Well, he farms out everything so all he needs to do is paint—one less paper to shuffle. My fear is he might interrupt his painting. I heard he might try his hand at pottery—something different. He was impressed with the terracotta warriors found in Xian when he visited China. If he doesn't paint, my great contract won't yield too much. And you know what happens when a favored artist changes mediums." He paused.

"What happens?" She questioned.

"We don't know! Sometimes it's successful, but more often a disaster."

They both paused, as if letting this thought mellow.

"Do you think I should go to his studio and speak with him?" She had strong reservations, but was relieved when Max told her Andrew never allowed people in his studio. When he painted, he wanted quiet and solitude.

Max described Andrew's retreat in the hills to her. There wasn't a house within a five mile radius from the studio. Andrew did have a friend, Leonard Small, who took care of all his electronics and was a bit of inventor himself. Apparently, he had invented some kind of food disbursing system, so Andrew wouldn't be distracted with cooking.

"OK, that's the first thing. A Power of Attorney. You implied there was more than one thing. So?" she asked.

He hesitated, and then spoke. "You know the property in Quebec we bought when you joined us? Well, I'm thinking it might be a good time to sell."

She interrupted. "You said about three to three and a half years. It's only two. What's the rush?" She was really curious. He was seldom wrong with the figures.

"It's about Peter Whitman. I'm going to share a confidence with you. Peter left—is leaving me, a sizable inheritance. He has stipulated that my inheritance will be based on the difference in my gross worth six years from the time he died. It was calculated, and will be again calculated at the six year deadline. I wanted to make sure my share of purchase profits will show up in my gross worth. The percentage I will receive is very generous, but if I don't increase my gross worth, I could get nothing."

"Come on, Max. Every year you get richer. It's impossible you'll get nothing. Well, let me give both these things some thought. I'll let you know when it all sinks in."

Chapter VI

*A*s Tammy left the building, her cell rang. It was Andrew Parks. He fumbled his words, as if tongue-tied. She heard him sigh, then start again. "Hi, Tammy. I was just wondering if you'd like to see my studio. I've acquired a new gadget and would like to show it to someone. I don't usually let people in here, but I think you'll understand. It's a work space, not a place for entertaining."

Tammy blinked her eyes. Max is never going to believe this one! She thought of the two experiences she had with him the previous week, and wondered what to expect of herself.

"Oh, how would I get there?" she almost mumbled, surprised at her own question.

"I'll have my friend, Leonard Small, pick you up. You name the time and place."

"Well, now is OK. I'm at the studio. There's a Starbucks across the street. How will I know Leonard?" She was now shocked at her answer.

"He'll have on a jean jacket and a hat with a floppy brim all around. I'll send him right away. It will take about forty minutes to get there. I've told him what you look like. What are you wearing?"

"Jeans and a baggy, blue sweatshirt."

"Great. He'll be there shortly."

As she shut off the cell, she thought, "I can't believe I did that." She did a mental check to see if she took all her meds. "Okay. Well, coffee time!"

She called her father and told him her plan to visit Andrew, just in case. Tammy was just finishing her coffee when Leonard arrived. He went straight toward her like a homing pigeon. "Tammy?" She nodded. "Hi, I'm Lenny—ready for a ride?" She stood up and picked up her bag. He was tall, broad shouldered and tanned. His blond hair was short and he was clean shaven. He guided her to a sport model BMW and opened the door for her. "Manners, in this day and age," she thought. Then she smiled. She could have gotten angry and said "Don't you think I'm capable of opening my own door?" What a paradox.

"He described you to a 'T'," he said without taking his eyes off the road.

"I thought he hardly noticed me," she cooed, playing an old feminine game from college.

He laughed. "You know better. I understand his eyes almost fell out when he met you. He said you were aloof at first, and then warmed a little when you met later on. I'm surprised he's inviting you to his studio, though. Very few people have been there. It's a sanctuary for him. Everything is arranged so he's never interrupted."

"I understand he has some kind of meal thing that prepares his meals." she queried. Lenny laughed. "Not quite. I designed the thing. It's a design with individual freezer units, each holding one meal. A code activates the section with the meal you want, described on a computer, then the meal comes out, conveyed on a belt to the microwave unit, which has a timer activated for specific meals, then a bell rings when the food is ready. The empty plastic plates and utensils are placed in the cleaning section, cleaned, ground, and placed in a recycle bin, which gets emptied monthly. Pretty cool, huh?" He had a broad, pleased smile on his face. Then he continued. "The food is automatically inventoried and monthly restocked so it doesn't get frosty. The unused dinners are taken to a food distribution center. Andrew had me include enough food for four people eating daily. He didn't expect to use that much, so it's one of his ways of making a donation and maintaining the dignity of the people. He really wants to show you his new toy. I don't know what you did, but you really had an effect on him."

Tammy was quiet. She was getting mixed up. Deep inside, she thought he was the one who killed her husband, yet the profile that was emerging didn't seem to fit.

They drove up a long driveway, and then at the gate next to the fence around the house, Lenny put his hand in a hole. The gate swung open. Lenny put his hand into another box about three car lengths up the driveway, closing the gate. "Entire hand recognition technology," he answered without her asking.

He parked the car in front of a section of building made with large redstone squares. It reminded her of the castle at the Smithsonian in Washington, D.C. They entered through a wide wooden door into what appeared to be a large hall. There were several easels set up along one side, each with what looked like an elaborate lighting system. There was a row of deep stainless steel sinks along the wall. Near the center of the room was a large apparatus with a chimney. There were tables with paints and brushes, some clean, some dirty. There were stacks of prepared canvases, and a section with a roll of canvas and equipment to make frames.

Andrew was on a ladder adjusting something near the top of the apparatus with the chimney.

"Having problems?" asked Len. "No, just making sure the chimney connection is tight." Andrew was climbing down the ladder as he spoke. He turned and came to them, grasping both Tammy's hands and looked in her eyes and said "Thanks for coming. Thanks for coming." He smiled, then let go of her hands, as if he became aware he was treading in her space.

When he touched her, she waited for her body to react, but nothing happened. His hands felt warm and strong.

"So, what do you want me to do?" asked Len.

"Take the other car. I'll drive her home when she's ready."

"I've got it," replied Len. He turned to Tammy. "Have a great day. Be easy on him. He's a little shy." He smiled, gave a wave, and left.

Tammy turned to face Andrew. "Wow, this is quite the artist loft. I don't see your famous food machine."

"That's in another area. I have a mini kitchen over this way. There are also toilets and showers in this section." They walked together to an opening with automatic doors. They went through to a fully equipped kitchen, a counter with ten stools, and a large harvest table with chairs.

"The machine is over here. Have you had lunch?" She shook her head no. "Here, scroll this screen until you see something you like. Or put something in that space there and it will search for you."

She started scrolling through the menus until she found something that sounded interesting.

"Now what?" she asked. "Push the enter button." She did and the entire unit moved. Then she heard a click and the machine moved her entrée toward another machine, which she figured was the microwave. Andrew made a selection and another entrée moved, but went to a different opening in the microwave unit. "It can take up to four dinners at one time in separate units. We can add more, but I have no use for more. Four is more than enough," he said as he shrugged. The bell rang, and Tammy's meal rolled out to a stainless steel tray. A knife, fork and spoon set-up dropped onto the tray. Then Andrew's food followed the same pattern. They put their food on the table, and went to the drink section. She selected an orange juice and he filled a glass with water.

Chapter VII

The food was very tasty. "This is very good," she said.

"It's all right for what I want it for. If I get lonely, I go out to eat or call Len to join me. Mostly, though, I'm working. I love to paint. Have you ever painted?"

"Awhile ago I did. I haven't painted for almost five years."

"Why did you stop?" he leaned forward attentively with his question.

"That's a long story. Some other time, maybe. What about you?" It was her turn to lean forward.

"I started painting in high school. I had a great, encouraging teacher. He suggested I go to Paris to study. I did. I was there about two years, then came back and started art school. In school, my sophomore year, I was very influenced by a painting by Tamila Anderson. She had won the 'Artist of the Year' competition and her painting was hung in a special honorary section for the winner, where it stays for a year before the next junior wins the prize. I went almost daily to study the picture. It looked different each time I saw it. It was a masterpiece. I never met the artist, and often wondered what happened to the painting."

Tammy was in shock. Then, almost in a whisper she said, "It's at my father's house."

"What's in your father's house? You mean Church?"

"I mean the painting you're talking about is in our family home, in the attic, I think."

Now it was Andrew's turn to be confused. "How? What? I don't get it."

"My maiden name is Anderson. I am the Tamila Anderson of whom you speak."

Andrew's jaw went slack and his mouth opened partially. After a long silence, he said, "I can't believe this. This is—wow—unexpected! Why is it not hung? Why aren't you painting?"

"I spent a lot of time with the art critic Professor Hubert Cox my last year. He taught me that everything about my pictures was wrong. My so-called modern impressionistic style was out-of-date, and questioned why my painting was hung so prominently—unless, he said—if it was being used as a perfect example of what not to do and how not to paint. By the end of the year, in this toxic atmosphere, I learned to hate my own paintings and my preferred style. Upon graduation, I brought my paintings home to store them and not look at them again. What I once saw as beautiful, now looked ugly to me. I wanted to stay near art, and was lucky to get the job at The Gallery." Tammy sighed. The tears in her eyes were a symptom of relief. She had never told her story to anyone, even her father. A prisoner inside herself became free. She was silent as her shoulders shook.

They just sat in silence for a long time, Tammy with her head bent. Andrew got up and brought a box of tissues to the table, waiting until she was ready for them. When she lifted her head, Andrew pushed the tissues toward her. Tammy blew her nose and started to come back to life.

"Another one—another victim of critic Hubert Cox. Well, at least he got his due!" Andrew was speaking in a soft, throaty voice.

"What do you mean?"

"Don't you know about the student suicide?" His question had a tone of surprise about it. "It was in the Alumni Journal and in a lot of the newspapers."

"I cut myself off from anything that had to do with the school. The mail went into the garbage and when I got married, no mail was sent to me. I told my father to destroy any mail from the college, no matter how important it seemed. So what happened?"

"It was the year you graduated. Two of your classmates tried to commit suicide. And one was successful. He left a detailed note, with quotes from the Professor. He said his actions, his control of his classes, made it impossible to get away from him. He said the Professor convinced him he was such a terrible artist that he should not take up any more room on earth. I guess he taught self-hate very effectively, implying that his targets should get rid of themselves. There was a lawsuit, but there wasn't enough evidence that he had, in fact, committed murder, but he was no longer allowed to work with any kind of students or any formal criticism. He murdered dreams."

"So I wasn't the only one. God help all of us!"

"What's sad to me," continued Andrew, "was that I saw your genius. Then to have it squashed out of you. What a loss."

Tammy felt exhausted, "How about a rain check for the rest of the tour? I think I'd like to go home and rest." Then, with a weak little smile, Tammy got up.

"Sure, of course," answered Andrew. "Tomorrow?"

"I guess so. Pick me up at noon. If I change my mind, I'll call you." She added to herself, "Always have an exit strategy." Andrew drove her home in silence, giving her the space to absorb and digest the news.

Chapter VIII

Tammy didn't call, so Andrew was there at noon. On the way to the studio, Andrew asked what Tammy was going to do with her prize-winning painting.

"I don't know. I haven't thought about it."

"How about selling it to me?"

Tammy was quiet. Then she answered. "This is all new to me. What do you want to do with it?"

"Hang it in my studio for inspiration. I'd like you to see it again and re-evaluate your work, and consider my opinion, that your work is the work of a talented and creative artist."

She thought a minute, then offered, "How about I lend you the painting?"

Tammy smiled. She hadn't thought about herself as an artist for a long time. She was curious how she would view her own work,—curious, very curious.

At the studio, Andrew shared his works in progress. He was working on four different paintings at the same time. His work still seemed ugly and unpleasant to her, but she did not report this reaction to him. He showed her two bedrooms near the studio. He explained how he would sleep when he was tired and work when he was rested. He explained that he seemed to have highly creative periods at around 3AM, but there were no real patterns. There were other more conventional rooms in the main body of the house, which were mainly unused.

"This is my newest toy," he announced. "It's just been installed. It's a giant kiln. I want to try to develop life-size pieces. It's easy to work. All I have to do, after putting my piece in, is flick these switches. These gauges measure the temperature, and this trolley is designed to make it easy to put a heavy piece in the kiln and place it in this section here." A large door opened and he demonstrated how the trolley worked.

Tammy was getting bored. She wasn't interested in any of the process, nor was she ever interested in the medium. Andrew looked at her.

"Not interested?" he asked.

She laughed. "You caught me. Not my thing. Once you create some pieces, though, I'll be real interested when I sell them."

He smiled. "Well, this design has taken awhile to get this far. I've got some ideas I want to try out but there's more work to do before I start." He looked up at the kiln. "I'm really proud of this baby."

He turned to Tammy. "So when will you paint with me? I'm asking you on a painting date. Pick your easel and I'll set it up for you."

"No, I don't think so. That's over. No, that part of me is over."

"Don't be so sure," smiled Andrew. "So what do I need to do to get your picture?"

"I'll call my dad and tell him to let you take what you want. Then you call him and make arrangements with him yourself."

When Tammy got home, she called her psychiatrist. It was time to explore her painting, her reactions to Andrew and review her medications. Then she visited The Gallery. She studied Andrew's paintings—seeing them as if it were the first time.

Chapter IX

Six months later, Max called in Bill and Tammy to tell them the news. "The buildings in Quebec have been sold—at a great profit." He looked at his picture of Peter Whitman and smiled. Tammy smiled at his smile, as he continued. "Also, last week Alice Gibson hung her 'Ascension of Mary' and we have been invited to a special party in Andrew Park's and our honor. She is very pleased, and so are we." He grinned again at Peter's picture.

Tammy hurried out of the studio. As she got to the gate of Andrew's place, she put her hand in the box. The gate swung open. She moved the car up and put her hand in the next box, closing the gate. She let herself in the studio and went to a bedroom and changed her clothes. She put on a smock, and hurried to an easel. It wasn't long before she was painting, intense and focused. Occasionally she would look up to see her college painting on the wall. It seemed to act as a motivator for her. She painted for several hours, occasionally stopping to drink water or juice. Andrew was the only one who knew she was painting, and was pledged to secrecy, even from Leonard Small.

After she showered and dressed, she examined her work. Then she looked at Andrew's work. It was hard to tell who did what. Their styles and technique were very similar. Andrew and Leonard would be on holiday for another week. She thought they might end up in England, but she wasn't sure and didn't care. She was spending more and more time at the studio and less time at The Gallery. Andrew had become a cash cow and Tammy was viewed as being related to his productivity. Before he went to Europe, Andrew had signed a Power of Attorney over to Tammy so she could transact his art business in his name. As Max had predicted, it made the transactions of painting sales effortless.

While preparing to leave, Tammy's phone rang. Andrew was excited. Leonard had just been offered an opportunity to head up a lab of inventive engineers in Germany, experimenting with a wide array of technical challenges, just what he likes to do. He would remain in Germany. Andrew planned to go house shopping with him and then would come home. She was pleased for Lenny, and wondered how Andrew would handle him not being around. They seemed to be really close. She shrugged. Not her problem.

For the following week she painted with more and more energy, and for longer periods of time. She painted her angers, her fears, her memories of her husband, her hate for Professor Cox. She tried painting the bearded man, but stopped because her own painting frightened her.

When Andrew returned, all she wanted to do was paint. He wanted to paint with her, but he couldn't keep up with her. She hardly slept. She became aggressive and hostile toward him. The only time she visited The Gallery was to drop off an 'Andrew' painting. She was now sleeping at the studio and seemed to get more and more agitated. Andrew was worried.

She told Andrew he was right. She was a genius. She was one of the greatest. She told him she visited the stars for energy and inspiration. Then she started to see shadows moving in the building. At first they frightened her, but then she said she was invincible, and they couldn't hurt her.

Andrew found an empty prescription bottle in the bathroom. When he handed her the bottle, she said she didn't need any medicine, she had her painting. Andrew didn't know what to do or who to call. Her father? Max? Who? He hoped he might get clues from her about whom to contact for help. Then, she seemed to calm. She talked slower and become more cordial.

While in Europe with Lenny, Andrew shared how much he had grown to care for her. Lenny was not surprised when he would say, "I'm the one for her—she's the one for me." He bought a ring in Amsterdam and had it specially designed.

She said she was going to visit The Gallery and would be back around suppertime. He smiled. She was her old self again. He'd have about five hours. He ordered in dinners from his favorite local restaurant. Flowers! He wanted flowers—lots of flowers. He disappeared into the house and came back with a dusty bottle of wine. He set the harvest table with crystal glasses, silver and dishes from the main house. The food arrived in special warmers and flowers filled the dining area. This was the night! He put the ring in the center of her plate. The black velvet box, cradling the ring, looked perfect in the center of her plate.

While Tammy was driving back to the studio, she was seeing shadows again. This time, she could see they had beards—chasing her car. She was driving too fast for them to catch her. She was hiding in the waves. She thought of Andrew. He's nice. He couldn't be the one. Old fearful feelings were emerging. She felt the car was full of waves. They couldn't see her because of the waves. When she arrived at the studio, Andrew greeted her with a broad grin. "I've got a surprise for you. Come to the kitchen." He felt pleased. The set up was nicely done. The ring was on her plate. The turkey sat in front of Andrew's plate, the carving knife and giant fork ready to use. She looked around at the flowers and watched Andrew as he poured the wine. He handed her a glass, then poured a glass for himself. "A toast—to us. I know you're the one for me. I'm the one for you." He took a sip of wine. She looked at him. "You're the one?" she asked. "Yes, I'm the one. I know you've known it these past months. I'm the one." She nodded. "So you're the one?" As she looked at him, his eyes drew dark, and he grew fangs. She was no longer afraid of the man in the beard. "So you are the one. At last I know."

She walked calmly to the table and picked up the carving knife. She walked over to the smiling Andrew and plunged the knife in his chest. Andrew's eyes went wide before he fell. Then she started plunging the knife into his body, again and again. She wiped off the knife and cut off a piece of turkey. She set out a meal for herself and ate dinner and had a few sips of wine.

"Ah, a woman's work is never done." she mumbled. She walked over to the kiln and opened the door. She dragged Andrew to the conveyer system and put him on it. She seemed very strong, lifting him easily. She pushed the second button and heard a swooshing noise. She waited until she saw the temperature gauge start to climb. Then she proceeded to clean up some of the kitchen, but did a poor job.

She showered, changed her clothing and drove to town. She went to the hotel bar and ordered a drink. She heard a voice that sounded familiar—the voice of Professor Hubert Cox. She turned, and the voice came out of the body of a young sailor. As she looked at him, his face changed into the face of Professor Cox. The voice was being rude and critical to the waitress. She walked over to his table and said. "Hi, there. I was just wondering if you'd like to come with me for a drink." The sailor looked at her appreciatively, got up and threw some money on the table. "My car is this way," she said and led the sailor to the parking lot. They drove to the studio. As they walked in, he looked around. "Hey, is this some kind of warehouse, or something?"

"Want to play a game?" she asked as she took off her suit jacket.

"Yeah, I guess so. What do I do?"

"Take off your shirt." As she said this, she took off her blouse.

"Yeah, this seems OK."

"Do just as I tell you. Take off your undershirt and your pants." She removed her skirt as the sailor, grinning, did as he was told. "Step next to that big sink there. Face the sink. That's right. Now bend over so your head's bending into the sink." He could feel her press next to him and put her hand on his back. He felt a little pinch as the box cutter sliced his juggler, and as he started to push up, he felt a pinch on the other side. He slumped into the sink as the blood flowed down the drain. "Goodbye, professor. All gone. You were a nasty man. Now you are out of my life."

She took a shower and went to bed. "Ah, I can rest at last." she sighed smiling to herself, then fell into a deep, restful sleep.

She woke up abruptly. "Things to Do! Things to do!" She jumped up, strong and full of energy. She went to the kiln and shut off the heater. She cleaned the kitchen, and got rid of the food and flowers in the regular garbage. The compactor reduced everything to a small block.

Then she moved the sailor to the conveyer system. She pushed the button and the door opened. A massive blast of heat entered the room. As the body moved toward the kiln, she threw the sailor's clothing on top of the body. When the door closed, she pushed the button and again heard the swooshing sound. "There—that's better! Much neater!"

She went to her paintings and picked two. She signed them, mimicking Andrew's style and used his name. She put them in the car and drove to The Gallery. She brought them directly to Max's office, knocked and entered at Max's invitation. "What do you think?" she asked. Max examined the pictures.

"The paint's still wet."

"Yes, he just finished."

Max kept looking at the paintings. "Something is different. I can't put my finger on it. More uncontrolled, more hurried, maybe. Maybe we're putting too much pressure on him to produce. What do you think, Tammy?" He asked as he looked toward the woman.

Tammy studied the pictures. "More unrestrained, more freedom is what I see. It's an effective change in style. The genius of the artist is finally showing." Her voice was sure and confident.

Max shrugged. "Unrestrained. Freedom. Genius. Maybe we can use that in the marketing. Well, you do the paperwork, since you're his official negotiator. We better let them dry before they get damaged. Good work, as usual, Tammy." Max returned his focus to his desk and Tammy left the office.

Chapter X

Tammy already in a hyper state grew even more tense and excited. She felt as if she might explode. Her senses were acute. She could hear tiny sounds unnoticed by most people, but seemed overwhelmingly loud to her. She felt if she jumped off a building, she would fly. Everything seemed to be moving too slowly.

She got into her car and zipped down the road to the highway. Faster! Faster! Turning curves. Rolling, Glass Breaking! And then, blackness—total blackness!

When she woke up, Bill was sitting next to her. She had restraints on her wrists. Her head felt foggy.

"Where am I? What happened?"

"You had an accident and an episode. I guess when they tried to treat you, you were very agitated. I brought in your psychiatrist. There was no trace of your medications when they took your blood levels. You should be balanced by now." As Bill answered in his usual direct style, he was alert to see if Tammy understood what he said. She did. She knew she was cutting back on her meds, which she thought was cutting into her creativity. Everything was a mishmash—jumbled—fantasy and reality mixed together.

"What kind of accident did I have?" Her voice was husky and soft.

"Automobile. You must have rolled the car three or four times. Seat belts and air bags saved your life. They had to cut you out. You car was mangled."

"Am I hurt?" she asked, trying to sense her body but she just felt numb all over.

"I don't think anything major. You're bruised all over your body. You have a purple face. You nose will be very sore, as will be some other parts of your body." Tammy's eyes fluttered, and then closed. She needed more rest.

Chapter XI

She had been out of the hospital for two weeks. She waited in the psychiatrist's office and was anxious to tell him how lethargic she felt. Yellow and purple marks replaced the blue. They talked. Her memory was fragmented. She held back some of the scenes she visualized. Mainly, she wanted to get out of this numbing fog that swirled in her head. "Too many meds," she told him.

The doctor agreed. She had been very ill, very aggressive. It might take awhile to get the successful balance they had in the past. "It's important to take the meds. Don't go off them." She heard some things and not others as he talked. "I've made a slight decrease in two of the meds."

She had the new prescriptions filled. It was another week before she became aware when one day started and another began. The paperwork was settled and she got a new car. She finally went to The Gallery, with everyone seeming very guarded when they talked with her. She thought she remembered bringing in pictures. She sought out Max.

"Yes. You brought in two of Andrew's pictures. There were parts that weren't dry yet, so we put them in the dry storage area. They are still there. You were in bad shape, you know. Power of Attorney is no good if you're dead." Max's demeanor seemed strange to Tammy. Was there something more than concern there, or was it just a trickle of her paranoia coming back?

She went to the dry storage area and studied the pictures. She looked at the signatures and had flashes of her signing his name. She examined the picture closely and looked in the upper left hand corner. There it was! A hidden letter A, for Anderson. She did that with all her pictures, known only to her. It wasn't a B, for Burroughs, but her maiden name initial. She looked again at the painting and knew it was hers.

Chapter XII

She drove to the studio. The kiln was off. The place was clean. She found a pile of clothing in the bedroom. There was what looked like a large dark brown spot on her bra. Tammy held her head. Those thoughts—those fragmented thoughts. Could they be just bad dreams?

She heard "Professor Hubert Cox is no more. He got what he deserved. Free at last. Free at last. God, almighty!" She vigorously shook her head to stop the voice—her voice.

In the kitchen, in the middle of the empty harvest table, was a black velvet box. She opened it to find a beautifully designed ring, original in style. She looked at the inner band to read the tiny engraving. It said, "I'm the one."

She sat down and put her head in her hands. "It can't be true. It can't."

She got up and walked to the kiln. It was full of ashes. There were clumps of metal mixed in with the ashes. Belt buckle? Coins? Dog tags? No! There was a blinking light on a control panel near the machine. The screen read, "Automatic shutoff engaged. Push enter to reset."

She went back to the kitchen. The compactor was empty. Then she realized if anything had been there, it would have been picked up by an automatic disposal chute that went somewhere. It could be picked up without disturbing anyone or coming through the gate. "No way to check," she thought. "No way to see if there was a knife."

She thought of Max. Did he suspect something? Should I tell my father? What do I do?

She drove home. Her father was staying with her since she came home from the hospital.

"Dad, I've got a problem and I want you to help me."

Chapter XIII

"What is it honey?" Charles was very attentive.

"Remember when you were on surveillance you had some kind of secret listening device you used when you were tracing a drug distributor? You said it listened, was voice activated, and recorded conversations."

"Sure, I remember. That was a big case for me. The recording clenched the case." He smiled, remembering some of his past glory.

"I need to get one of those units and I want you to show me how to use it."

Charles looked at her, wondering what she was up to now. Then he spoke. "The good ones are very expensive."

She gave him a cutting look.

"OK, OK, I forget you have lots of money. Well, you also need a court order."

"I just want the device. Can you get me one and show me how to use it?" Her head seemed clear and her thinking was racing.

Charles looked at his daughter and knew about her determination. He also knew she wasn't going to share more information.

"I guess I could get you a unit. It will take awhile, since I suppose you want top of the line equipment."

"Yes—and the bugging unit needs to be as small as possible." Her voice was intense and firm. "And," she added, "As soon as possible. I don't care about the expense."

It was three days later that Charles arrived with a box containing the equipment. He laid the recorder on the dining room table, checked the unit, installed the battery, and then called Tammy on the phone. "I've got it. I'm at your house now. Swell. See you in twenty minutes."

Tammy examined the equipment. It seemed simple enough. Charles said, "The closer the receiving unit is to the mike, the better quality recoding you will get."

"Will it go through walls?" asked Tammy.

"Yes," answered her father. "That's what makes the difference in price. It is dependent on what the wall is made of. Some walls will block the transmission."

Once she felt comfortable operating the unit, she looked up, her face soft and warm and said, "Thank you, Dad. You've been more help than you would ever believe." A tiny tear formed in one of her eyes and she turned away.

It was very late when she went to The Gallery. The night watchman seemed surprised to see her. "How are you feeling? I heard you had quite an accident."

"I'm doing well now. It's time for a little catch-up." She nodded toward the bag she was carrying.

"If you need anything, give me a call. You know where I'll be. I'll be making rounds in another hour."

"Thanks. See you later." As the guard turned down the hall, she went straight to Max's office. She took the tiny microphone and stuck it behind the picture of Peter Whitman. It looked like a velvet pad put on furniture to keep things from scratching. Even if seen, it was unlikely to be recognized as a microphone. She went to her office and set up the receiver system. The signal unit flashed 'on' and the signal indicator showed a strong signal. She put the unit in her desk drawer. The indicators remained in the 'to go' position. She completed everything in less than fifteen minutes. She locked the desk.

She called the guard and asked him to join her. He came to her office and she told him she wanted to surprise Max with some flowers and asked him to join her in Max's office to see where he'd suggest she put them. She asked him to sit in Max's chair, and scan the room. She had him make comments from different positions, and he suggested a place near the window on a small table to put the flowers.

"You've been very helpful. Thanks." The guard left and got ready to make his rounds. Tammy checked the machine. The voice activation worked. Their conversation was crystal clear.

She left The Gallery feeling very satisfied. If Max was suspicious of anything about her, she was sure he would tell Peter Whitman about it.

Chapter XIV

It was the evening of Alice Gibson's party. She had postponed it until Tammy felt better, and Andrew had not responded to the invitation. Max called Tammy and asked it she had heard from Andrew. She told Max she thought he had gone hiking in the Rockies, and his cell phone seemed out of order. She said he often went off by himself for long periods of time for inspiration.

The party went well, although Alice was very disappointed that Andrew was not there. During the evening, Tammy shared that she had found several paintings in Andrew's studio. Max seemed to relax at the news of more paintings.

The next day, Tammy stayed late at The Gallery. She was anxious to check the recording device. Was Max suspicious she was substituting paintings?

After several uninteresting entries, she heard Max's voice address Peter Whitman.

"Peter, I need your help. I'm not sure what to do. I know I messed up not killing Tammy, but it's not too late. I still have six months to go. I still don't know how she got away. The insurance will go to me and Bill, as the partners of The Gallery. Bill doesn't have a clue. Here's my dilemma. She is doing great work with Andrew. And she has the Power of Attorney. If I kill her, we could loose control over Andrew. The insurance would really increase my gross. Send me a sign of what to do, old friend. I'll be waiting."

Tammy was dumbfounded. Max didn't have a beard. Insurance, yes. Nigel had mentioned something about it. It was coming back. He had insisted all three partners be very highly insured in the event one of the partners dies. He felt Bill was at highest risk, since he was the oldest, with Tammy being lowest risk because of her age. The surviving partners would be the beneficiary of the policy.

"So," Tammy thought, "If I died, not only would Max get the insurance money, but increase his inheritance from Peter. But why did he kill Nigel? He wouldn't have inherited any of the money. And", she thought, "what about the beard? The man who attacked me had a beard. So you want a sign from your old friend, do you? You will get your wish!"

Chapter XV

Tammy was neatly dressed in a style Max loved. She had learned a lot about him during their discussions together. She knew what he valued and was confident he would be interested in what she planned to suggest.

They met in his office. She sat in the seat familiar to her, a reminder of their good times together. He'd often end their session with "Great discussion, really fun."

Max looked alert, curious about what Tammy wanted to talk about. He looked over at the table near the window. "Thanks for the flowers. It adds a nice touch. So, what's up?"

Tammy smiled. "I have an idea you might be interested in. It's a business proposition more than anything. It involves your inheritance from Peter Whitman. You're in the last six months of the final tabulation, is that right?"

Max sat on the edge of his chair. "Yes, that's right. This is the home stretch." Max said with focused attention.

"Well, I am sure you know that Nigel left me a very wealthy woman. If you married me, your gross worth would increase significantly. Why not get that extra money? We can worry about me taking a small share later on. In truth, I've been very appreciative of the things you taught me, and it seems like an effortless way for you to increase your income."

Max looked at Tammy. Married—to a young, wealthy widow? It never crossed his mind. She really did get his lessons. Finally he spoke.

"It's a brilliant idea. The business end makes wonderful sense. What about the married part? Will we be—married—or will this just be business?" Max was almost holding his breath.

"I don't think you find me unattractive, and I do have my own needs, so I think we could be really married and make it work."

"I—I thought you had a thing for Andrew?" questioned Max.

"Please, Max. Compared to you, he's just a boy. I've got money. I want intellectual challenge and the wisdom of someone older than myself."

Max looked at Peter's picture out of the side of his eye. Then he got up, went to Tammy. He knelt down on one knee, took her hand and said, "Tammy, will you marry me?"

"Yes, I will." answered Tammy. She learned over and kissed him on the forehead. They both smiled.

The wedding was small, and held at Alice Gibson's home. Alice was enthralled and loved fussing. Her staff did all the work, but the way Alice described things, you'd think she did everything herself. Alice told Bill and Janet Buxton that she was rather glad that Andrew did not respond to the invitation. She thought Andrew was attracted to Tammy and his appearance may have made things awkward.

They flew to Paris for their honeymoon. Alice Gibson had arranged for a hotel suite as a present. Alice did have good taste. The suite was lovely and the service exceptional.

They settled in their room, and then went out for dinner. When they returned, it was early evening.

Max took off his jacket, not quite sure what to do. Tammy poured them both a glass of champagne, a gift of the hotel. Then she said, "Congratulations!" and tapped his glass with hers, then took a sip of the drink. "I have a little present for you." She said, and took a small package out of her purse. Max tore off the wedding paper, opened the box and found a minute recording device.

"It's wonderful what they do with chips these days. No more tapes. There's something recorded on it just for you, Max." She was smiling.

Max put the tiny earpiece in his ear and pushed the button. As he listened, the color drained from his face. He shut off the machine and looked up. "You know!" he gasped. "Then why?"

"It's still good business, Max. And I knew that insurance policy would be an important magnet. In fact, you could still do me in and collect both ways. That's why I have three copies of this recording in the hands of people unknown to you. If anything happens to me, they will be properly distributed. So, Max, as soon as we get back, let's get the paperwork done so it shows an increase in your gross worth. The deadline will be here in no time. I do have some questions. Why did you kill my husband?"

Max's shoulders were slumped. After a long silent pause, Max mumbled "It was a diversion. If he died, the focus would be on him, as it was. You would be incidental. If it was only you there might have been more attention to our policy."

"What about the beard?" Her voice had an icy tone in it.

"It was a disguise. I didn't expect anyone to see me with so many houses closed, but if someone did, they'd be looking for someone with a beard. And it worked. You always thought about the beard. It was a perfect distraction."

"Thanks for being so honest with me, Max." She kissed him on the forehead and said "Let's get some rest. There's a lot to see in Paris."

Chapter XVI

The inheritance to Max from Peter Whitman was massive. Tammy continued to 'discover' paintings at the studio. As Tammy brought a painting to the gallery, Max stopped her. He looked closely at the painting. "This painting isn't very old. Andrew has been away longer than this paint is old. What's going on?"

Tammy smiled at Max. "Everyone thinks he's away. And he is away a lot. But having a lover who's far away isn't much fun, is it? He loves to paint. I like to watch him."

"So you're having an affair with Andrew!" Max was angry.

"Of course not. He isn't here. How could I have an affair with a man who isn't here?"

That night, Tammy reviewed a book on poisons. She knew an internet search could be traced. When she went to The Gallery the next day, she proceeded into Max's office. She turned toward Peter's picture and said, "Peter, I have a problem. I'm having fun torturing Max, but I don't know what I should do. Should I poison him first, then tell him I'm getting the partners insurance, or just tell him I was thinking about poisoning him and let him worry. What do you think, Peter?"

Tammy's cell interrupted her musing. "Hi Tammy, its Leonard. How you doing?"

"Leonard!" Tammy's heart skipped a beat. "How great to hear from you. How's the job going?"

"I'm having great fun working about a hundred hours a week. I can't seem to get Andrew, though. Did he get a new cell number? The number I have says it can't connect me."

"Not that I know of. I have the same problem with the number I have."

"Well, when you see him, tell him to call me. What's new with you?"

"I'm married. I just got married."

"Great! How'd you like the ring he designed?"

"I loved it. Len, it wasn't Andrew I married. I married Max, from The Gallery."

There was a long silence on the other end. Then he said, "He really loved you. What happened?"

"I don't know. He got moody and went rock climbing someplace. I haven't heard from his since."

"Did he propose to you? Did you say no?"

"Yes, on both counts." She waited.

"Did he leave after that?"

"Yes, the next day, I think."

"I'll bet he got depressed. That sounds like him. He's done that before. I mean, run away when he gets deeply disappointed with something. No telling where he went, or for how long. I really wanted to talk with him."

"I was in a car accident. Totaled the car!"

"Wow! Did you get hurt?"

"Just bruised and banged up a little. I was real lucky."

"Well, if he ever emerges from the black lagoon, tell him to contact me. I think we're onto something in the alternate energy field. I thought he might like to invest in the project. I guess it would be fruitless to come home. I'd never find him. I'm still surprised you said no to Andrew."

"It was a little too much, too soon. I've know Max over four years."

"Well, if and when you see Andrew, tell him to give me a call. Do you have my current number on your screen?"

"Yes, I've got it."

"Good. Store it, so you can give him my number when you see him. It was good talking with you, and congratulations."

That night, Tammy dreamt of Andrew rising out of a black lagoon. He had the face of the monster who she remembered chased her. She woke up in a cold sweat, shaking.

She went down the hall to Max's room. Max was sleeping soundly, making little grunting noises. She said, "Max—Max" softly as she shook his shoulder. Max opened his eyes and looked at her.

"Max, I want to say I'm sorry. I've been treating you poorly!"

Max was puzzled. She had been treating him poorly, but he expected that. He wasn't expecting this gentle behavior.

"I think we're missing some good opportunities—you and I together."

Max reached out to her and gave her a hug. "Come," he said. "Just lay beside me and I'll hold you. Nothing more. Let me hold you."

Tammy slid into the bed next to Max. He put his arms around her and they snuggled together. They just laid there, both awake, both thinking.

Chapter XVII

One of Tammy's meds was making her sick to her stomach, both at night and during the day. She visited her doctor and after reviewing her blood levels, said she was right on the cusp—a little less might not work and a larger dose would be toxic. He was concerned that if she wanted to try a lower level, she would need to have her blood checked two, maybe three times a week. She disliked the blood draws, but disliked getting sick more. They made appointments for the blood draws.

Tammy wondered if it was the medicine that was helping, or if she was just temporarily in a remission. She wondered what would happen if she had another episode.

She called her father and said she wanted to talk with him. She was worried that she was becoming less and less interested in things. Painting had become less satisfying. The Gallery, once a place of joy and excitement, was transforming into an unpleasant place to visit, and the tasks that were fun now seemed like unwanted chores.

While at her father's house waiting for her Dad, she went to the attic and dug through the pictures she had painted in college. She now looked at them through her professional experienced eye, rather than the eye of a woman badly damaged by a sadistic professor.

Some of the paintings were amateurish. She could see her skills evolving as her experience grew. Most were interesting, and nothing special. She would have rejected them all for display in The Gallery—all but one. It was the one she did just before the prize winner. If she were an art teacher, what would she suggest this person do to develop their talent? She heard her father come in the house and she went down the stairs.

"Hi honey," he said and gave her a hug. "Cup of tea?"

"Sure, Dad, sounds good."

Her father put on the water kettle, took out two cups and put tea bags in them. He left the cups by the stove and sat down at the kitchen table near where Tammy was sitting.

"Feeling OK?" he asked.

"A little flat," she answered.

"It's been bothering me. Why did you need a bugging device?"

"I thought Max was saying bad things about me. I needed to know if it was real or paranoia. I married him, so I guess it was all right." The kettle screeched its readiness. Charles got up and poured the water into the cups and brought them back to the table. Tammy looked at him. "What really happened to Mommy?" she asked.

"She got sick. Went to the hospital and died."

"Not good enough Dad. I really want to know what happened."

"All right, you're a big girl now. I know you know bits and pieces of her story. It started when you were born. Your mother had a bad case of post-partum depression. She called me at work one day and told me to come right home—there was an emergency. When I got home, I looked around. Nothing seemed unusual. I asked her what was going on. She told me she almost threw the baby out of the window. Actually, twice—she went to the window with you, and stopped, both times. I took a leave of absence and stayed home with her. We went to the doctor. He said depression hits a lot of women after birth. I was afraid to leave you alone with her. I called my mother, who was alive then, and asked her to stay with us awhile. She did. Your mother started to feel better and my mother went home. Then one day the house was full of bags, stuff purchased from several local stores. She seemed real energetic, up and happy. Most of the items she bought were useless to us. A couple days later we took much of it back. There were days I would come home in the evening and she'd be sitting in the dark, smoking a cigarette or holding her head up with her hands, with her elbows on her knees. Sometimes, when she was feeling up, she'd get flirty with my friends, like she was horny and had no control. Other times she would have dark moods and talk about dying. She'd have no interest in anything. She'd stop going to her sewing circle and quilting group, which she loved. There were periods when she was down she had difficultly reading, and that would make her feel worse."

"Did she ever hurt anyone?"

"She tried. Usually in an up period she would be happy, energetic, and feel she could do anything, but sometimes she would get intensely angry at nothing. During these times I couldn't trust her. She almost ran someone down with the car, on purpose. It really scared me. I took my guns and left them at the station after I found her one day trying to get into my gun cabinet. She wanted to shoot a dog that annoyed her. When I took the guns away, she said she'd now have to use a knife."

Tammy blanched. Her father noticed. He looked lovingly at her, "Are you sure you want me to go on?"

"Yes, Dad, I need to know."

He continued, "There were the dreams. She would dream I was some kind of monster she had to protect herself from, and hit me with the lamp or whatever was handy. I kept all my tools locked in the cellar to protect myself. Then she had a real bad case of depression. She wouldn't get out of bed and would soil herself in it. Or, she would go out in just her pj's and walk toward the highway. That's when she was hospitalized. Somebody brought in a birthday cake for a patient and she stole the knife. That night, she killed herself." He was quiet for a moment. "The doctor said this kind of illness runs in families. That's why I worried when you were under a lot of stress. I know you see one of the best psychiatrists around and you take your meds. Just keep taking them. I don't know what I'd do if I lost you." He had tears flowing from his eyes. Tammy couldn't remember a time she saw her father cry. She gave him a hug. She found herself consoling her father, thinking that this was certainly a reverse role. They both cried.

Chapter XVIII

Max was surprised to find breakfast waiting for him. Tammy never prepared anything for him, not that she wasn't capable, it was just her way of punishing him. He was living a single life with a female roommate and existed on basic greetings to each other, cordial professionals. Max stayed quiet as he sat down at the table.

"Thanks for last night," she said. "It was nice being with you. I've been thinking about my conversation with Leonard. He asked me why I married you rather than Andrew. Whatever were our reasons, what I told him was true."

"What did you tell him?" asked Max.

"I told him Andrew was too much, too soon, and that I've known you for over four years. And I thought of the things I said to you when I made my suggestion that we get married. I am impressed by your logic. I really enjoy our discussions. You murdering for money certainly influenced how I saw you. I know it's like the old joke,—other than that, Mrs. Lincoln, how was the play?"

Max was quiet. Then spoke, "What I did was stupid, unethical and illegal. What I considered doing, especially about the insurance, falls in the same category. It's like a sickness. I go crazy—never being satisfied with enough money—no matter what I—we have. Look how much money we have. I'm still nickel and diming artists who can barely pay for their paint. And I'm good at it! I can negotiate contracts that others would never attempt. It's a thrill to win—then on to the next race."

"Max, when you say you don't have enough money, you know that's crazy talk. Why don't we treat it like the sickness it is? What if you had professional help to look at the dynamics?"

Max was quiet again and started picking at his food, now growing cold. "You won't have to tell them that you actually killed someone. Just say you've thought about it. That's extreme enough."

"But about us!" he protested. "You know I've killed someone—someone near and dear to you—and you know I've even planned to kill you! That's a little detail that might be a sticky point in our relationship together. I'm already thinking of ways to get to you without jeopardizing myself!"

"Yes, and we will both, not just you, but both of us continue until one of us is dead or in jail. Max, that is no way to live!"

"What do you propose?" Max was engaged. They were both getting into the swing of the discussion the way they did when they had their mini seminars.

Tammy rolled her eyes up in thought. "Well, I think we could start over. Let's plan a honeymoon date. I know you like deadlines, so between the time we leave and the time we agree to do this, you do two major things. One, see a psychiatrist, and two, court me. Be romantic. Woo me. Sweep me off my feet."

Max laughed. "I don't think I know how. In this area, we're both amateurs. Why not! It might even include something we both know little about—having fun."

She smiled. "You did propose once. When do I get a ring?" Max laughed again and started developing a courting plan.

Chapter XIX

During that day, she was excited about their discussion. She drove out to the studio to look at her prize winner. Once inside, she looked around and thought a good investigation of the place would tell lots of stories she didn't want to be told. She examined her painting closely. She could see the subtle difference of her improvement and would, indeed, hang it in The Gallery. It was quite good. She thought of that fateful night. She only remembered fragments, but one thing she knew, she had been very crazy. She could not afford to ever get there again. She thought of her dad's plea, "Take your meds."

On her way home, she stopped at the real estate office of a woman she knew from The Gallery. They greeted each other warmly. Tammy explained she was interested in Andrew Park's property and was managing some of his accounts. She asked the woman what would be necessary to buy or sell the property. The woman took down as much information that Tammy could provide, and told her she would get back to her in a couple of days.

Tammy arrived home to find flowers in the living room, kitchen, bedroom and main bathroom. On the dining room table was a printed invitation.

"Dear Mrs. Pennington

You are Cordially Invited to Dine

with

Mr. Maxwell Pennington.

A car will arrive to pick you up at 7:30 PM this evening."

Tammy looked at her watch. It was three-thirty.

A stretch limo pulled up at exactly 7:30 PM. Tammy looked like a model showing high-end clothing when she walked into the restaurant. The restaurant was on a hill overlooking the bay. A waiter had been ready to escort her to a private room. As they passed through the regular dining area, Tammy felt admiring looks from both men and women when she walked by. As she entered the private dining room, Max stood up. He looked with total admiration at his 'sort of' wife.

After a carefully served and wonderfully tasting dinner and before desert, Max took a small, plain box out of his jacket. He took a modest looking diamond ring out of the box and took her ring finger. "I don't know if this will fit." The ring slipped on as if it had been sized for her hand. "You are now officially engaged," smiled Max. Tammy looked at the ring. It didn't seem to fit the style Max would choose, and it looked lovely on her finger. Max spoke. "This is serious stuff. That was my mothers ring."

Max and Tammy had breakfast together again the next morning, but this time they ate before they started talking. "Well, another new experience. Thank you, wife!"

"I love my ring," Tammy said, looking serious. "You shared a lot yesterday and we took on some real problems. Now I have some to put on the table. I want you to know that the last six paintings I brought in weren't painted by Andrew Parks."

Max looked startled. "Someone else did them? Why? Who?" Max was confused.

"You noticed the paint was new the other day. I implied that I did, and I didn't see Andrew, and you suspected I was having an affair with him. That's what I wanted you to think, to make your world more bitter. I haven't seen Andrew since just before my car accident."

"Then who is doing the paintings?" asked Max.

"Me. I'm the artist. They are my paintings. I've been passing them off as being done by Andrew."

"We're in deep trouble" grumbled Max. "Andrew will sue us for selling forgeries as his paintings."

"No, he won't. First of all, the agreed sale price went into his escrow account. Second, and more importantly," she hesitated, "he, Andrew, is not alive."

"What do you mean, not alive." Max was confused and puzzled.

"He's dead. That's what not alive usually means." She wasn't smiling.

"How do you know he's dead?" Max was doubtful.

"Because—because." She stopped then started again. "I was crazy. I killed him."

Max stared at her in disbelief. "So, that's our problem for the day," she stated. "So you see," Tammy said, "I'm not as pure and innocent as you thought. We both have something to hide."

"Is there anything else I need to know?" gritted Max through his teeth.

"Yes, there is one other little thing. That same night I killed Andrew, I killed a sailor. In my craziness, I thought he was Professor Hubert Cox. It all happened during the same episode."

Chapter XX

Max was visibly shaken as they drove toward the studio. He needed to see everything, especially if they were going to see this through together, and it was taking him time to absorb the gravity of both their situations.

"This is quite a set up" he noted as they drove in. "How did you get such access?"

"I did what you told me to do, get close to Andrew. I think he was head over heels in love with me and gave me anything I asked of him. Yet, I was pretty sick and suspicious during that time. I thought he was the monster with the beard that had chased me." As she said this, Max squirmed a little. "He got me painting again. It was a wonderful gift." She parked the car and they went into the studio. Max kept thinking he had a lot to learn about this woman he thought he knew.

Tammy led the tour around the area and described what she knew. She showed him more of her paintings and described the Professor's story. Max listened intently. He liked her prize winning painting and almost seemed to be proud of her school success and became angry at the Professor.

Max asked Tammy about the rest of the house, and was surprised to find Tammy had never been through it. "Let's explore," he suggested, and they went through a hallway to the main house. It became clear that the studio had been an add-on after the main house was built. It was obvious from the dust and cobwebs that the house had not been used for some time. Room after room had beautifully carved wood, doors and frames. There was almost no furniture. It was a house of old elegance. The kitchen had pantries and a dumbwaiter. Near the far side of the house was a small section that had been used more recently. There was a bedroom, a kitchenette, bathroom and sitting room. It was furnished, the bed made, men's clothing in the closet. The refrigerator was plugged in, but it was empty, except for some bottles of water.

"Leonard Small! I'll bet this is where Leonard Small stayed. I often wondered where he went." Tammy acted as if she had solved a puzzle.

On the way back, Max commented. "It's a beautiful house, especially the wood. The kitchen is pretty dated. It was made for a lifestyle of another era." They drove in silence most of the way home. Max had a lot to think about. Tammy wondered if she had shared too much. They both appreciated the silence.

Chapter XXI

Tammy called the doctor to report that the nauseous feelings she had were disappearing and to also check the results of her blood level and medication. "Everything is in the normal range," reported the nurse.

"I feel I'm in the normal range, too." she said to herself, amused at her own joke. She had been thinking of taking Max on a surprise little trip when she realized she was constrained to the local area because of the blood draws. She thought, "A new kind of restraint." She was wondering what she would need to do if she went on a trip, when the phone rang. It was Ellie Brown, the real estate agent.

"The property you are interested in is not owned by Andrew Parks," she reported. The owner is a—hold on. I've got it right here. The owner is a Mr. Leonard Small. I was unable to contact Mr. Small. I was told he is out of the country." Tammy thanked Ellie for her efforts and hung up her phone.

It rang again. It was Janet Buxton. She sounded hysterical. "They took Bill. It was bad. I'm at the hospital. I don't know what to do, Tammy. He's had a heart attack. I couldn't reach Max."

"I'll be right there, Janet. Just hold on. I'm on my way." As Tammy drove to the hospital she rang Max. No answer. She left him a message about Bill and where she'd be.

Janet's eyes were red, her face swollen. Tears kept rolling down her cheeks. "Bill's never sick," she moaned. "Oh, I'm so worried. He grabbed his chest and fell. I called the emergency number. They came and took him away. He didn't say anything. They just took him away. His face looked twisted. Oh Tammy. He's all I've got. He's all that matters to me." Tammy held Janet in her arms as she sobbed with deep heavy breaths. Tammy patted her back gently and said nothing. She wondered if anyone had thought of giving her a sedative.

A man in a white coat came through a swinging door. "Mrs. Buxton?" Janet stood up straight and turned to the man and asked, "How is he?" The man dropped his eyes. "Mr. Buxton is no longer with us." Janet's legs started to buckle as Tammy caught her. The man quickly moved and assisted her, steering Janet to a nearby bench.

"Can you give her something?" Tammy asked the man. He nodded yes and went back through the swinging door. He returned with a nurse and a wheelchair.

"Are you family?" asked the nurse. "No, we're friends."

"We'll take care of her," said the nurse and turned. They assisted Janet into the chair and rolled her away. Tammy stood there, trying to process what just happened. Then, as if waking up, she went through the door. "She can't be alone. Don't let her be alone!"

Bill Buxton had been well-liked. The reception line at the funeral parlor flowed out into the parking lot and down the street. Janet's eyes were glazed. There was a frozen smile on her face as people streamed by mumbling things she didn't hear, but nodding her head as if in approval. The mob was passed on to family members, some with the same nodding, smiling behavior, but none whose eyes were glazed like Janet's.

On the drive back home, it was clear Max was deeply touched by Bill's death. They had been friends a long time. Bill also had been instrumental in navigating Tammy through some bad times. "Nigel was right," mumbled Max. "Bill was the first to go. Somehow, I never expected it. I miss him already." They were quiet the rest of the ride home. Unspoken were thoughts of the people affected by death and their own roles in the drama of life and its ending.

During the next few weeks Max took charge of decisions at The Gallery usually made by Bill. He promoted Susan Stone to an Associate Director and told her to hire a replacement for her job as Administrator. Family members were staying with Janet, who had become a living zombie. She seemed to appreciate Tammy's visits, but Tammy felt that Janet's unresponsiveness from the haze of medications made the visits seem long. She had a new appreciation for what Bill had done for her during her own personal crisis.

Chapter XXII

"That new woman Susan hired seems like a quick learner." commented Max.

"Susan herself is also proving herself," added Tammy. They looked at each other.

"It feels like the pressure's off for awhile. How about we take a little break?" asked Max.

"Like what?" responded Tammy without looking up as she examined a new canvas.

"Like getting back to courting." He smiled. "Madam, would you accompany me to hear the Symphony play Beethoven this weekend? If you say no, I'll have to find someone else. I already have the tickets."

Tammy looked up and smiled. "I'd be delighted to accompany you, Mr. Pennington." She reached out and squeezed his hand.

The insurance company settled the claim from Bill's death. This was followed by a notice of a massive rate increase if the remaining partners wanted to be covered. "Maybe this is a blessing in disguise," said Max looking at the notice. "What do you think?"

"I think it removes motive, making life easier." Tammy's voice was soft, and a little tight.

"Motive, yes. Now we have to also find a way to remove evidence. We could have problems with Andrew's studio." Max was pensive.

"Oh, in all the excitement, I forgot to tell you what I found out. Andrew Parks didn't own that property. It belongs to Leonard Small, his friend."

"Isn't that the man who called you from Germany looking for Andrew?"

"Yes, that's the one. He was working on some kind of project in alternative energy and thought Andrew would be interested in investing in it."

Max listened carefully, then tilted his head to the left, a habit he had when he was problem solving. Max jumped up. "Do you have his phone number?" he asked.

"Yes, on my cell."

"Good! Call him. Call him now." Tammy pulled out her cell and dialed.

"Hi. Leonard here." his voice was crisp and clear. "Hi, Len, this is Tammy."

"Hi, Tammy. This is great. You've got Andrew's number? This deal is ready to pop."

"No, I don't have Andrew's number. My husband, Max, wants to talk with you. Max, this is Len," she said into the cell, and then handed it to Max.

When Max got off the phone, he was smiling. They had talked for a long time. "I agreed that we would purchase the property the studio is on, and then Len will use the money from the sale to invest in the alternative energy project. That's it, in a nutshell. Lots of details to cover, but that's the end result."

"You mean, the studio? We're buying all that land and the house?"

"Even better. He said we should destroy the kiln. He told Andrew it wasn't safe. He was afraid it would blow up and someone would get killed. I assured him that Andrew would be provided a place to paint and to stay, if he needs it. And the big surprise—Len is Andrew's half brother—same mom, different father."

The concert was a delight. Tammy had a chance to show herself off and Max was glad to have her on his arm. Beethoven was a favorite of Max. His enthusiasm for the music was caught by Tammy, who had much less exposure to classical music than Max. On the way home, Tammy asked Max if he ever played an instrument. Max grinned. "I used to play sax with a group in high school. I thought I would get more into music, but college was about business and money. My dabbling in art was from a business perspective, not like you. Your heart is in art."

"Art for me was an escape," said Tammy. "I could hide in painting, painting out fears, joys—any kind of strong feelings. I went to art camp a couple of summers. I spent a lot of time at the museum. I was a junior docent, a kind of go-for job for the adult volunteers, and I liked it. I realize now my folks tried to get me away from the house as much as possible. All the craziness just seemed normal to me."

Max asked, "How did you like our date?"

"It was great, Max. I'm starting to relax with you and just enjoy what we're doing."

"Well, be ready for a new adventure tomorrow at noon. Dress comfortably, and use walking shoes."

"Max, what are you up to?" she was smiling.

"I'm courting." He grinned.

The next morning, Max put a cooler in his car, then opened the door as Tammy came down the steps. "Your chariot, madam." he said, making a deep bow. They drove to a large park near their home and parked next to a picnic table. Max beckoned Tammy to join him on the path, and then reached out for her hand.

"Where are we going?" she asked.

"For a walk." responded Max.

"I mean, walking to where?"

"Just walking," said Max. "Wherever our feet take us."

She wasn't sure she believed him. "Just a walk? That's not like Max," she thought. She wondered what surprise he had in store for her, so she decided to just go along with his plan. They followed a path that made a big circle and brought them back to where they started. Max brought the cooler out of the car and set up a picnic lunch on the table. They ate. They chatted. They noticed the birds and flowers. When they finished eating, Max packed up the cooler. They drove home. "A walk and a picnic." she thought, "How quaint!"

Chapter XXIII

"Max and I want to go away for about a week, but I don't know what to do about the blood draws. Is there a way we can go out of the area? I know how important maintaining my meds are, but I feel a little trapped, with draws two days a week. Is there a way to manage this?" Tammy was pleading. The psychiatrist nodded his understanding. "We're lucky we're doing two a week, not three. When you were in the hospital and in an acute state, it was about two or three times daily. I think we're in a good range now. Are you having any unusual symptoms? Anything, like an upset stomach?"

"The only thing different is that I feel stable, not too moody. That's unusual!" She didn't know if she'd get a smile from him, and she didn't. He remained very formal.

"You make your plans to go where you want. I'll prescribe extra pills in small doses for you to bring with you. While away, you can have your blood drawn at almost any medical center and have the results faxed to me. If your levels indicate changes, I will let you know right away and you can take what you need wherever you are. If you feel you need a local doctor, let me know where you're going and I may be able to recommend a colleague, but I don't expect that will be necessary. What's critical is that you must have a way for me to reach you."

"That's good news. How are things going with Max? Do you think you can help him? I guess you know I recommended you."

The Doctor paused, then said "You ask Max about that. I don't discuss patients with anyone."

"Even his wife?" Tammy was surprised.

"Even his wife." This time he did smile.

As Tammy entered the house, she heard soft music, with an occasional squeak. She followed the sounds to find Max playing a saxophone. He looked up and said, "I got to wondering if I could still play. It's coming back, but slowly." He put the sax down, got up and gave her a greeting hug. This was new, and she liked it. They both sat down.

"I can go away for our honeymoon. The doctor told me how we can handle my meds. Where do you want to go?"

He looked at her. "I like a city. Boston, New York, Montréal, San Francisco, any of them would suit me fine. If you want an exotic island, we can do that, too. What's your pleasure?"

"I like the city idea. They all have more art than we can see."

"Boston then," stated Max. "It's not too overwhelming, and it's easy to get to everything."

They both checked their calendars and chose a date. Max was visibly excited. Tammy smiled at his excitement. It was beginning to feel nice to see his excitement, different than experiencing pleasure from his pain.

The paperwork regarding the sale of the property had begun. Tammy had told Max she wanted Ellie Brown to help so she could earn a commission. It was a good choice. Ellie was detailed and thorough and knew the real estate business. Max got permission to remove and destroy the kiln before all the paperwork was done. Max supervised the job himself, and had the stainless steel sinks removed along with the kiln. He stayed with the workman until he saw the kiln and the sinks being crushed in an auto disposal yard. He came home and expressed his relief. "I have the perfect place to celebrate."

"Do I need to dress?"

"No, very informal."

As they drove, Tammy tried to find out where they were headed, but all Max would say was he was courting her and wanted her to be impressed. It was about a half hour later when Max drove into the driveway of a farm. There were two silos and signs all over advertising items and food for sale. Max waved for Tammy to follow him. They walked into a small building, painted white, then into a kitchen-like set up with tables and chairs all around for easy access. "Here we are!"

Tammy started laughing. This was not on her expectation list.

"What kind? Cup? Cone? Sundae? I'm having a butter pecan cone, just plain." Max was grinning like a little boy.

"Strawberry. I'll have strawberry. A cone. The sugar cone, please."

They walked around the store, looking at little novelty items, tee shirts and hats, all for sale. Max found a small ceramic vase. "I think this was made in a kiln." He offered it to her. "A gift for you, my lady. May we be thankful for this important day."

Chapter XXIV

"What if we started an art school?" Max wondered. "We could have it for select students who could compete for scholarships. There would be tax advantages as well, I'm sure."

"That could work. I'd want to take down the entire studio, though. Too many bad memories."

"That wouldn't be too hard. It was an addition on the side of the building and could easily be restored."

"Are there any people we should see or buildings we should look at for ideas when we go to Boston?"

"I don't know. Let me think about it." He hesitated. "I don't want Boston to be a business trip. That doesn't fit into my courting and seduction plans."

Tammy smiled. "When did you add in, seduction?"

"Just now. You approve?" She nodded a yes. Both looked like they just heard a funny joke.

Max was in his brainstorming mood. "Back to work. Lots of property. We don't have to make a decision now. The ideas will come. A school is a big commitment. I think a better question is what kind of lifestyle do we want to live? How do we want to structure our time? How do we manage The Gallery? Then we can see how the property fits into our plans. We've already accomplished our main goal with the property. My next goal is to enjoy Boston!"

Chapter XXV

The Boston weather was pleasant.
The boat ride view of the city seemed
romantic to both of them.
The wine.
Her naughty nighty.
His last reservation expressed, "Any small packages?"
Her answer: "If I had one, it would play the music of *Revel's Bolero*."

Chapter XXVI

The next morning while walking down Boylston Street, looking in the shops, they heard the shouting. Someone was running down the street with a gun, a policeman following behind with his weapon drawn. The man turned, and shot the policeman in the shoulder, knocking him back and dropping his gun. People were scattering and diving thru shop doors. Max moved toward Tammy to pull her aside, but Tammy stayed fixed, her eyes on the man running toward them.

"It's the Professor," she gasped. The man was running straight, oblivious to the people around him. As he ran past, Tammy put her foot out, clipping the man's leg. He fell forward, banged his face on the sidewalk, with his gun sliding down the street. Max jumped forward and retrieved the gun and aimed it at the man.

"It's him, Max. It's Professor Cox!" The man scrambled to his feet and looked at Max who had the gun aimed at his forehead. She wanted to yell, "Shoot! Shoot!" but she didn't. Then she said, "Don't shoot, Max, don't shoot!" The wounded policeman caught up, holding his gun in his right land, his left arm limp. It seemed like only seconds later the street was filled with police cars and flashing cameras. A visit to the station-house, paperwork, a lot of appreciative thanks and the event was over.

"I didn't quite get what he had done and was running from," said Max.

"I don't want to know and I don't care. He shot a policeman. My father was a cop. I know what will happen to him."

Max was quiet for a moment. "When you said it was the Professor, I was going to shoot. Then, I must admit, I considered you might be wrong. I was relieved when you said, 'Don't shoot.' I'm not sure what I would have done if you said, 'Shoot!' Well, you're a hero," he said.

Before they left Boston, they bought wedding rings. There were no rings involved in the marriage ceremony since it was a 'modern' wedding—a business arrangement, a way to get revenge.

Something had happened. Something new and clean was emerging for both of them.

Chapter XXVII

When they returned home, Max spent the next several days reviewing The Gallery books and in meetings with Susan Stone. Max then met with Tammy. He had a briefcase full of papers, inventory sheets, charts, graphs, and all his usual resources when he made a plan or negotiated a contract. "Tammy, what would you think if we gave up The Gallery? Well, not all of it, but not work here. We'll turn the entire operation over to Susan. We'll hold our own mortgage, and Susan will become the owner. If she defaults, it comes back to us. Part of our agreement would be to function as consultants for three years, with decreasing commitment of time each year. It's a good tax plan for us, and frees us to go and do whatever we want."

Tammy was quiet. Her head whirled. This had been like a pleasant home for her the last several years, a stable anchor in a stormy life. "What would I do?" she asked out loud, more to herself than to Max.

"I thought you might like to study art in Paris or wherever you want."

"What would you do? This place has been your life."

"I want to learn more about music. Oh, I don't mean become a performance artist, I'm too old for that. Music for me allows me to float off, like you do with painting. I guess what's appealing to me is to do something I was really interested in, but unable to do because of circumstances. We have a freedom that few people have. We're learning a new way to be with each other. Maybe we can learn a new way to be with ourselves."

She looked at Max. He looked different. She felt different with him. This was not the man who stalked her. This was her husband. This was the man who knew she could become crazy at any time. She somehow felt protected by him, not frighten of him. She thought of Janet Buxton and the joy she had being with Bill, demonstrated by her behavior at his departure.

"Interesting. Interesting idea. All this is too new. I need to let it soak in some. It has possibilities."

Later, they both were sitting reading, when Tammy said, "I know what I want to do with my share of the insurance money. I want to make a restricted gift to fund the mental health center at my art school."

Max looked up. "Sounds like a good plan. We can use the deduction. Do you have any ideas about the property?"

"No, not yet, unless we want to make it into our own home."

"I don't think it would pay. Too many improvements are necessary. I was thinking it might make a nice '55 and over' planned community."

"Oh Max, what about the school idea? Scholarship kids for art studies."

"And music," added Max. "Everything is on the table. No plans yet."

"I've been thinking about your suggestion of studying art someplace. This mental health stuff is also interesting to me." Tammy mused.

"What about studying art therapy—using art to express hard-to-express feelings!"

Max watched Tammy snap to attention.

"That might be interesting, very interesting. We could start a residential community at the property for kids who need special help."

"Good," laughed Max, "As long as they take accounting. Kids nowadays can't even count."

"Maybe you could find a kid to mentor like Peter Whitman found you."

"Oh, I forgot to tell you. Next Friday night I play with the band at a real gig—some kind of office party. I'm the only one in the group who's not a doctor. When I met them, I told them I wasn't very good, and they laughed and said I was a lot better than my predecessor."

The phone rang.

Tammy was surprised to hear her father's excited voice. "I've had a surprise visit from a man who wants to hire me as a detective to help him find his half brother. Tammy, it was Leonard Small! He didn't know we were related. I told him I met his brother at a party at The Gallery and you were my daughter. Mind if we come over tomorrow and speak with you? It seems you were the last one to talk with Andrew Parks. Maybe between the three of us we can figure out where to start looking for him."

Tammy stared at the phone. "Uh—sure! I'll ask Max to be here, too. How about 11 a.m.?"

There was some mumbling in the background, then Charles answered, "Great! See you tomorrow!"

Both Max and Tammy looked tired when they sat together with Charles and Leonard drinking coffee. Tammy noticed the age difference between Max and Leonard seemed greater than she remembered. Tammy repeated what she had told Leonard on the phone, that she had said no to his proposal and he left, mumbling something about mountain climbing.

Leonard put his head down. "I'm sure he was devastated. I only hope . . ." he broke off and looked around at the three others. He sometimes gets depressed. He can get real moody. Not often, but when he does get down, I worry about him. It doesn't usually last this long for him to bounce back.

Max looked at Leonard. In a soft voice he asked, "Do you think he committed suicide?"

Leonard put his head down again, nodding "Yes." Then lifting his head, stated, "And maybe not! He could be injured, had a memory loss, lots of things! That's why I contacted Charles to help me check—one way or another. Well, I know the area he usually climbed. I guess we'll check that out first. There's also a place on the west coast in California he liked to visit. It's famous for its hot tubs and relaxed atmosphere."

Tammy realized she really didn't know much about Andrew. He didn't talk while painting, and when he did, he was encouraging to her, not sharing about himself. It was only once he mentioned he rock climbed, and Tammy hadn't been very interested in him beyond their business arrangement.

When they left, Max hugged Tammy. She was shaking. "It's okay," he whispered. "They're gone, nothing to worry about."

That night, she could feel herself getting agitated. She was to have a blood draw the next day or did she miss one? As she went into the bedroom, Max looked as if he had a beard. His eyes were dark. She said, "Max, I'm getting sick."

Max picked up the phone. "Why are they whispering?" she asked. "Come," urged Max. "They'll see us right away."

"Who are they? Is this a trick?" Tammy was getting upset.

"The doctor Tammy. Your doctor. To check your meds." Max was worried. He was feeling helpless as he watched her behavior change. She started to get tremors.

"Are you trying to poison me?" she yelled.

Max picked up the phone again. He spoke quickly, and then nodded, as if the party on the other end could see him. "Tammy," he spoke softly.

"Let's go down and have a cup of tea. Come. We'll put the kettle on." Max walked slowly toward the kitchen. Tammy followed. Max put on the tea kettle and took out two cups. He thought a moment, then brought over four boxes of different teas. He suggested she choose her own tea. He didn't want her to imagine he was trying to poison her. When the kettle whistled, he poured the tea. There was a knock at the door. Two men and a woman, each carrying a bag, came in. "Hi, Mrs. Pennington. We've come to take your blood levels."

Tammy picked up her tea cup and threw it at Max. "You're a traitor." The woman drew a syringe from her bag. Tammy yelled when the woman stuck a needle in her arm, as the two men restrained her. It wasn't long before she was asleep.

She woke up in the hospital bed. Max was sleeping in a chair next to her. She turned toward Max and called his name. Max woke up with a start, sitting at attention.

"Hello Max. I had an episode, didn't I?" Her eyes looked sad.

"Yes. It wasn't too bad. What do you remember?"

"I remember getting worried, feeling anxious, talking to you, someone holding me. Not much. Why is your hand bandaged?"

"I spilled some tea on it and got a little burn. Nothing serious."

"How long will I have to stay here?"

"Not long. You're in good shape now—you weren't that far off. I think you'll go home in a couple of days."

"Now you see how I can get. I suppose I'm more than you bargained for."

"Bill told me how he had to help once in awhile."

"Do you want—are you still going to stay with me?"

"Of course. The payoff to be with you is wonderful for me. You've changed my life. I expect a glitch now and then. Maybe we both need to keep track of your med schedule."

"I feel different. Did they change my meds?"

"I think so. This is the plan we had arranged in case you had a problem. It worked well. You have a different doctor, though. I think he made some adjustments to get a faster response so you could go home."

"It took a long time to get a regime that worked. I'm not sure it was a good idea to change my meds."

They released her two days later with instructions to keep her monitored at least two more weeks and to contact them if any major changes occurred.

"I feel out of balance, Max. Sometimes I have gaps, like a form of amnesia. I seem to lose time, yet I do see pictures, flashes of memories, with strong feelings."

"The doctor said to expect that. I can tell when it's happening. You just sit and don't respond too much. The doctor said that it will go away little by little, as you adjust to the medication."

"I don't like it, Max. I just don't like it."

They were about to have dinner. Max had his favorite brought in—turkey and all the trimmings. Max pushed Tammy's seat in at the table. Tammy smiled.

"You look more relaxed."

"Yes," answered Tammy. "I'm feeling pretty good right now."

"Want your turkey thick or thin? I like a thick piece myself."

"Not for me. The thinner the better."

As dinner proceeded, Tammy could feel herself drifting. Max watched as she got quiet and stopped eating. He got up and went to the stove for a cup of coffee. When he turned, she was standing next to him. She plunged the carving knife into his stomach.

"You're a bad man. You killed my husband." She let go of the knife and stood quietly for several moments. "I'm going to bed, Max. I'm tired." She walked away and went up the stairs to the bedroom.

Max slid to the floor. He reached in his pocket and pulled out his cell phone. He hesitated a moment, then pushed his 411 button. He whispered into the phone. "Intruder—with beard—stabbed me—need help." He gave his address and hung up.

He pushed Charles' number, "Tammy's not well. Need your help. I've been stabbed by a bearded intruder. Help her!" He dropped the phone, feeling dizzy. He reached a napkin and wiped the handle of the knife before passing out.

Max stirred. He could see Charles sitting next to him. Max shook his head, trying to clear it of the jumbled thoughts. He looked at the needle in his arm and knew at once he was in the hospital. Max almost shouted, "Why are you here? Why aren't you with Tammy?!"

Charles gestured with his hand. "It's okay. She's at home. Leonard Small is with her. She's quite worried. I convinced her to stay home if I visited and checked up on you. You've got a nasty wound. A guy with a beard—damn, I began to think she made that up. After her husband—again. Boy, that's a clue! Well, the police are on it. No prints on the knife. Front door unlocked. Not much to go on. Tammy was sleeping when everyone got there and was in a bit of a daze when she woke up. Said she was on new meds—made her sleepy. I convinced them to avoid interviewing her for awhile, based on her reaction to her last experience. Well, your wound is bad, but you'll recover."

After two uneventful days, Max got a fever that kept climbing and his pain severely increased. Somehow he had gotten a systemic infection that went through his entire system. Within the week, Max went into shock, and then, died.

Charles and Leonard moved in with Tammy. Her new doctor said he was pleased with the results of her meds, in light of the current stressful events.

At breakfast, Tammy looked at Leonard—healthy, handsome, young Leonard. She wondered what she would be like if she got manic when Leonard was around—a person that was already stirring strong sexual feelings within her.

PART II

Short Adventures

Gnawing Feelings

You'd never expect to find a place in the city that could be so quiet! No hustle, no bustle. A series of subway cars lined up, chrome glistening, shining orange seats, clean floors! That was different! The sick-blue water flowed underneath the empty cars—underneath the bridge where you could see the third rail glistening. The muted light gave the structure of the bridge and the city in the distance a silver-gray hue, yet the soundless wind curling through the superstructure gave no hint of the noises and aromas of the city in the distance.

From the perch on the bridge, cars in the lot next to a factory near an old and rotted pier seemed like toys, quietly lined up by a pensive child. The graffiti on the bridge's structure seemed to soothe its rough texture—while the wind blowing over the water seemed to agitate and make the water rough.

Still no sounds! The absence of sound had a sound of its own—a sound that had a taste of—dryness—the kind of dryness one gets when about to give a speech—dryness with a hint of saltiness. Could it be—the saltiness—a residue from the water below? Was this water mixed with salt water? Which way did the river flow? From this distance, it was impossible to tell by watching the water flow past the Brooklyn Bridge.

The gray buildings, the eerie quiet, the empty cars, the absence of visible life forms trigger a sense of loneliness. "The strange thing is, I wanted to be alone," mumbled the traveler to himself. Well, he was alone, here on the Brooklyn side of the river.

Should he go back, and climb down from his perch, or follow the walkway—heading to—*where*—across the river. Did he want to walk so close to the third rail, glistening and visible from this angle, but hidden, yet near, when walking the wooden planked path?

He moved, as if a force drew him toward the path. He climbed down, and then walked carefully on the wooden beams, looking down through the spaces between them, and then climbed onto the walkway. "Ah—on the path—a firm path—straight and direct to—to—." He had no idea. This path was not like his life's path, full of twists and turns, hills and valleys, and he was unclear of that destination, also.

He wondered about this path—its safety—its destination. It went straight as far as he could see, all the way across the expansive river. He noted the sun to see how much time he would have before it got dark. He noticed the gray clouds in the distance.

He picked up his pace and started walking briskly. He was young and in good shape. He unbuttoned his impeccably tailored suit jacket. His tie waved as if trying to escape the starched collar of the white, monogrammed shirt.

He wondered if a train would come to this desolate area, but he thought it would be unlikely. Soon the row of cars was far behind him and he was almost mid-way over the river when he muttered to himself, "Perhaps I shouldn't admit this, but this was a stupid idea." He was not used to acting on ideas he had labeled "Stupid." He was too precise, too methodical. He acted on information, not impulse. Data! Facts! Numbers! It had served him well. "What the hell am I doing <u>here</u>?" he thought.

What, indeed. He had felt like he was ready to blow up, an explosion building within him. He looked to the left, looking at that part of the city that had been his world for the past ten years since he had finished his studies at Worton. All the people, the noise, the numbness to others so he could be effective, were taking their toll.

Why did he drive here and climb to the train storage area? He knew of it when he and some investors took a tour with the Mayor, but why here? What was going through his mind? Why did he walk in this direction instead of returning to his car? Where was he going?

The sun peeked through the clouds. He caught a glimpse of his wingtip shoes, highly polished, moving in and out of his view, pointing—pointing ahead—pointing ahead to—where? Why was he here? Colors seemed to swim through his head as he pushed onward. The tenseness was unbearable.

He looked at the path in front of him turn into a tiny line. He could feel his determination build. This was a familiar feeling. Once he made up his mind to do something, the task would consume him until it was achieved. He now focused on the other side of the river, where he could now see the bridge link to the land. His already brisk pace increased, and he began to feel a bit more relaxed. Working on a specific all consuming task was a kind of meditation for him. It would clear his mine of everything else.

That gnawing feeling, the reason he wanted to be alone, stayed just below the surface, somehow connected, somehow driving him. Uneasiness, a conflict, unfamiliar to him, was emerging. A police station flashed through his mind, a court with jurors, the witness chair, the court stenographer, and then it was gone.

He neared the end of the bridge. The last half of his trip seemed to go quickly. No trains had passed him. The path of wood planks abruptly stopped as the bridge ended and the tracks rolled on, twisting and bending their way down toward a tunnel in a distance, a mouth swallowing the shiny sticks of steel.

He climbed down a metal ladder that ended six feet from the ground. He positioned himself so he could grab the bottom rung, swung down, and let go. He had been an outstanding athlete, and it showed in the way he landed on his feet, bending his knees, cushioning his fall.

He scrambled down an embankment and came to a street. He looked around at mostly warehouses, as if to get a bearing. He started walking to his left. He could feel his internal danger system alerting him. This was the wrong part of the city to be dressed in a business suit.

There was nothing in sight—no cars, no people, not even a dog or a cat. He came to an intersection with a street coming from the right. He could see traffic in the distance and turned up the street toward the traffic. About a block before the trafficked street, he passed two men sitting on a loading dock. As he passed, one passed a bottle in a paper bag to the other. He could feel their eyes on him as he walked briskly toward the traffic.

The autos and trucks zipped by behind the guardrails on the highway. The street running parallel to the highway started to show signs of life—people, children, bars, and an occasional store. There would be no taxis in this part of town! People he passed would stare at him as he continued down the street.

He saw a Salvation Army thrift store and hurried to it. He picked pants, a shirt, and a dungaree jacket and put them on. He carefully rolled up his clothing and put it in the shopping bag with handles the tired looking woman at the counter gave him. She scribbled the address of the store on a scrap of paper, as he requested, after she had given him directions to the nearest subway, about eight blocks away, and told him that only a local train would stop, and not too frequently.

He left the store feeling safer, yet aware his shoes did not match his costume. He came to a shoe store nestled between a vacant store and a barbershop. He pointed to a pair of running shoes when he realized the wrinkled old man spoke almost no English. The man measured his foot and brought a pair of shoes. The brand was unknown to him, but the shoes fit well and were very comfortable. The old man rang up the sale on an old fashioned cash register. The price showing in the window of the machine was about $1/5^{th}$ of what he was used to paying for his usual brand. He left the running shoes on and put the wingtips into the bag. The two men smiled at each other as he left the store.

He felt safer as he continued toward a subway entrance. A group of children were in a lot playing a kind of ball game with a pink ball and a broomstick handle. As he walked by, the boy at bat hit the ball high and long enough to bounce off the building at the end of the little field. The boy scrambled around the bases as another boy in the field attempted to catch the ball as it came off the building and missed it. After a scamble to get it, he threw it to a team mate as the boy ran past home plate. The runner looked at the man as he passed, grinning broadly. The man returned the smile and gestured a thumb up with his empty hand.

He found the subway entrance. It would be about a ¾ hour wait before he could get a train to Manhattan. He pushed the turnstile and went down the stairs. It was as if he had gone back in time. The station must have missed the last few renovations when they repaired the subway system. Darkness, broken tiles and graffiti surrounded him. The bulbs in the lamps that weren't broken could not have been more than twenty-five watts, leaving an eerie, yellowish cast to everything the light touched. There were no machines for candy or newspapers, and the place smelled of urine. The seats that were not broken were well worn, polished by supporting many bodies over many years. He sat down and waited, noting the time.

After fifteen long minutes, three young men came down the stairs on the other side of the tracks. They looked at the man and seemed disinterested. There was laughing, pushing and shoving and then two of the men exchanged jackets. Firm, muscled arms displayed tattoos of skulls, knives and chains. The taller man shook his head, and gave the jacket back to the smaller man. It seemed he didn't like the way it fit. They laughed again. The man looked at his watch to note the time. "About 15 more minutes", he whispered to himself. As he looked up, all three of the young men were looking at him—and his watch—his fancy watch. Everything grew quiet for a few moments, the young men whispered to each other, and then looked again at him. They walked slowly to the stairs and started up. The man looked around. No place to go! He ran quickly to the end of the platform and jumped down into the darkness lit only by train signals. He could hear the trio coming down the stairs. He saw a dark depression in the wall and pushed into it.

"Where the hell did he go?" Someone asked crossly. "Rocky, you look that way. We'll look this way." Two of the men went in the other direction and Rocky came toward him. He jumped off the platform and walked slowly in his direction, into the shadows.

"Anything?" came the voice from the other side of the platform. "Nothing yet," answered Rocky in a deep, rich voice. For the next long minute, the man felt he hardly breathed. "Nothing here!" came the voice from the other end just as Rocky looked directly at the man. The traveler knew Rocky could see him and held his breath. Rocky stared, then replied, "Nothing here either. I don't see nothin'—Come on, let's get out of here. We'll miss our train."

Rocky turned, walked quickly back to the platform and easily pulled himself up. He walked over to his two companions as they climbed up onto the platform. The man heard them climb the stairs and a moment later descend the stairs to the other side of the tracks. Within a minute, a train groaned to their side of the platform and stopped. The man could hear the doors open and close, and then watched it as it creaked away around a bend.

The man took a deep breath, pulled himself out of the depression in the wall and scrambled to the platform. He could hear the rumble of another train coming. He could not climb up as easily as Rocky, but with an adrenaline assisted effort, pulled himself up just as the train came into sight.

The train was almost empty and the ride was uneventful. He got out at a familiar street and walked to a hotel he liked to have booked for his out of town guests. The reservation clerk seemed to pay no mind to the way he was dressed and rang for a bell-hop. The bell-hop was about the same age as the man, and took his shopping bag. "This way, Sir," he said enthusiastically and politely. When they got to the room, he opened the door, put the bag carefully in the luggage area, opened the blinds and adjusted the thermostat. "Would there be anything else, Sir?" "Yes. Would you be able to have my suit cleaned and pressed right away?" The man pulled the suit from the bag. "No problem, Sir. Give me a couple hours. Anything else, Sir?"

"No, not now. Maybe later. I need to get settled first." The man gave the bell-hop a very generous tip. The bell-hop pretended not to look, but in a very discreet manner noticed the amount of the bill placed in his hand. Then he looked again as if to make sure he had seen correctly. He turned and said, "Please, Sir, if you have any needs, call the desk and ask for me. My name is Philip. I would be more than happy to serve you."

The man smiled. "Thank you. I will, Philip." He smiled again as the door closed and thought "Philip! Not Phil, but Philip." He was remembering a large life-sized cutout that was sold at an auction he attended. The cut-out was a bell-hop in a red suit with two rows of brass buttons down the front of his jacket, a round and flat red matching hat, holding a tray. The slogan, "Call for Philip Morris" was printed on the cutout.

The man made a call and arranged to have his car picked up. He took the scrap of paper with the address of the Salvation Army out of his wallet. He spread the paper on the desk, took a hotel envelope out of the desk drawer and copied the address on the front of the envelope. He wrote a check, placed it in the envelope and sealed it and placed it on the desk.

He showered, then called and asked for Philip. He instructed him to buy underwear, socks, shaving materials, and a white shirt. He wanted the items washed, and the shirt starched and pressed. They agreed on a time his goods and suit could be delivered and hung up the phone.

He pulled back the covers and plunked himself on the bed. As he started to relax, the gnawing feeling returned. He had been annoyed about being bullied into being a witness. He also felt the man's crime was being exaggerated, and that the prosecutor was making an extra fuss to set an example with this man. The man was not in much of a position to fight back. The arrogant prosecutor had chosen his victim well. He would be just another pawn to advance the prosecutor's career.

Although all this annoyed him, he knew that these kinds of things happened. It was something else—something he should know—something he should remember.

He closed his eyes and went into a sound sleep until a rumpus in the hall disturbed him. He stirred, and then drifted into a twilight sleep. It was then the vision came to him.

He was a little boy. He was noticing that the light that evening showed him something he'd never thought of before—how he took the light for granted.

They had waited for dark to sneak to the ship. It was to be a full moon. As they hid on the edge of the beach in a grove of trees, the sun set. They could see the boat that had been dragged up the beach past the tide line. He knew they were in grave danger. If they were caught, all their work would be destroyed and they may even be killed. They needed to escape.

The ship, anchored far out in the deep water would be a refuge if they could reach it. The captain would give them asylum—if—they could reach it. As the pink light turned to gray, the shadowy grove turned dark. Then the unexpected—clouds covering the moon! It became dark—a kind of dark he never experienced before. His father held his hand, giving him comfort. "It's too dark," whispered the woman. "No, dark is good," answered the man in a hushed tone. "Once we get into the water, we'll be able to see the light from the ship."

He gave a signal and they moved toward where they thought the boat would be, but they couldn't find it. It was a strange sensation, staring into the blackness and seeing nothing. Then a cloud got thin and let a hint of moonlight get through. They could see the outline of the boat before them.

"Hurry!" urged the man. "We'll be missed at bed check." The boat was heavy. All three pushed, but the boat would hardly budge. The man went to the back of the boat and lifted as he pulled, as the boy and the woman pushed the bow. The boat slide slowly, inch by inch, toward the water. They heard shouting in the distance. They could see three lights at an upper area above the grove of trees. "Quickly—push!" The man's voice was tight—anxious. The boat made a little scraping noise as it moved closer to the water. The back end of the boat touched the water. The noise of the water as it hit the boat seemed magnified. The boat was almost in the water when one of the lights came out of the grove and moved directly toward them. "Get in the boat!" whispered the father hoarsely. "Duck down."

The light came up to the boat, then flashed right into the frightened boy's eyes. A Far-off voice called, "Anything down there?" The light moved off the boy and a voice at the other end of the light boomed out

"Nothing here!" Then the trio could feel the boat being pushed the rest of the way into the water. As they floated out, they could see the light move down the beach. The boy shook violently as his mother held him in her arms and the father rowed toward the tiny light in the distance.

The knock at the door broke his trance. He was trembling as he let Philip in with the requested items. He tipped him without speaking. He did not want Philip to hear the quaver he knew would be in his voice.

It was the next day. The man was back in court, this time on the witness stand. The prosecutor was rambling on, and then turned toward the man. By now it was clear he was the main—no, the only witness to the alleged crime. The prosecutor dramatically swept his arm as if to include the entire courtroom, yet lingered his motion as he pointed to a tiny man, drawn and pale, thin hair, sitting behind a table in the front of the courtroom. "Do you see the person who committed the crime anywhere in this courtroom?"

The man looked directly into the eyes of the frightened figure behind the table and answered, "No, no one here. I don't see anyone I recognize here." He smiled to himself. The gnawing feeling was completely gone. He felt whole again.

Transformation

Ralph could feel he was deteriorating. He could not walk without getting angina, nor could he dance to a fast beat. The last time he tried, he was at a wedding. After finishing up a slow dance, the music changed to a wild and intoxicating beat. Ralph could feel the music flow through him and started to move. The more he moved, the more the music flowed through him, the more joy he felt. He was smiling, almost in a trance, when the pain hit. It was like a stone on his chest, and his jaw became tight.

A little embarrassed, he told his partner he had to sit down, then put the nitroglycerin tablet under his tongue. In a minute or two, his jaw relaxed and he was able to breathe more easily. The tightness in his chest was subsiding. The nitro worked—this time.

He wasn't frightened; he was annoyed—no—angry about this limitation. He loved to dance, and now that special pleasure was no longer available to him.

It was about a week later when Ralph heard an Indian healer talking about transformation and the power of the mind. He talked about changing physical reality with mind power, letting go of attachments, and the oneness of all living things in the universe.

Ralph decided to concentrate on transforming his physical reality. To run, jump, and move quickly without pain was his goal. He meditated, did relaxations and visualizations all on the same theme. He worked on letting go of things and attitudes that he considered an attachment, and felt he was making progress.

One night, while lying on his left side, he heard a very rapid pulse beat in his left ear. He tried to time the rate of the pulse, but it was too fast for him to get an accurate count. He rolled on his other side and listened for a similar beat, but all he heard was his normal pulse, about 70 beats a minute. He took his pulse on his wrist, and it, too, was 70.

Ralph rolled back to his left side and again heard the rapid pulse. Over the next two weeks, Ralph continued to check as he did the first night with similar results. At a routinely scheduled appointment with his doctor, Ralph shared the phenomenon.

"Probably something going on in your inner ear. If you'd like, I'll refer you to our ear specialist," the doctor said flatly and without emotion.

"No, not yet," replied Ralph. "It causes no discomfort. I only hear it when I put pressure on my ear with the pillow." The pulsing continued, and Ralph just accepted it and no longer became distracted by the beat.

Ralph's transformation work with his body continued. He read more of the transformation concept. He kept his focus on running, jumping, and moving quickly without pain.

It was a hot, muggy Sunday afternoon at the end of July. Ralph was in his backyard moving some wood from one part of the yard to another. He felt a little dizzy and sat down under a tree. Everything started to get blurry, then turned gray. After a few moments he saw a flashing bright orange light. He started to open his eyes. The light of the day seemed very bright.

He focused on his heart beat. He could feel it beating, but not its normal rate. His heart was beating at the very rapid rate he had been hearing in his ear.

He looked down at his hand and was startled to see a gray paw! The other side was the same. He looked around at himself. His body was covered with gray fur. He even had a bushy tail!

He looked around. He was in a tree! He looked down and saw his body slumped to the ground. He thought of his transformation affirmation—to run, jump, and move quickly without pain.

He scrambled from the branch to the trunk of the tree and easily ran down the trunk. He examined his old body in amazement. He realized he had achieved the result he had worked for, but this was not what he had expected to happen.

Suddenly, he had the urge to eat. It seemed to be an all consuming force. He ran toward the birdfeeder, jumped onto a limb of a tree nearby, then to another branch, next nimbly landing on the birdfeeder. All memory of his former lifestyle faded. The only thing on his mind seemed to be food. He ran, jumped, and moved quickly, finding food and running from predators.

The Musings of Ralph

As he visited his dead friend in a funeral parlor, Ralph mused about him.

"He has left his mortal home. His body had served him well. The passage was completed as he passed through that place that opens into bright light.

Did I really see something lift from his form? Did I really see a mist reach out and merge, a guiding cloud of accumulating energy disappearing through a pinhole of light?

Could it have been just a reflection of the prism of the crystal in the stained glass window? Could it have been the shadows playing tricks with my imagination?

This I know. The house he lived in is empty. I no longer feel his warmth. What is that? Oh, it's a crow signaling me its time to fly."

Ralph nods a good-by, glad for the connection he had. He knew the existence of his friend had changed him, and that awareness was within him only, unless he choose to share it.

Ralph went to his car and just sat there for a few moments. He could hear his breath go in and out, his chest rising on the intake, lowering as he released the air. He sensed a slight tightness between his shoulders and the lower part of his neck.

The sun was low in the sky, peeking from behind the trees, shafts of light finding their way thru the maze. The colors around him changed, and he was bathed in the orange and golden glow of twilight.

He smiled as two young boys, about 9 years old, passed by the car. As they walked, Ralph watched their shadows dance before them, long and gray on the sidewalk. "My shadow has grown long, too," he thought, "Except it is on the other side of my life. Their shadow is just beginning, and will grow short, then long again. I've already done that. I wonder when my sun will set."

He thought of Mable, eyes closed, breathing noisily, lying in bed in the nursing home. He had been holding her hand for what seemed a long time when her breathing became more labored. Did he really see Mable get up out of the bed as her body stayed still? Did he really hear her share a few of the significant emotional events in her life with him in a clear crisp voice—the labored breathing fading in the background as her voice became clear and strong? Did a shaft of light enter the room that was no longer a room, but a field full of yellow roses, her favorite flower? Was there really a path thru the flowers leading to the shaft of light? Did he really hear her say, "Well, it's time to go. I'll come visit now and then for tea. If you pay attention, you'll notice when I'm there. I'll bring my own cup." Mable walked down the path and looked back as she reached the edge light. She turned, smiled and gave a little wave with her right hand. There was a yellow rose in her left hand. Her bed clothing had transformed into a soft, glowing robe emitting a light of its own.

She lowered her hand, turned and moved into the light.

Everything faded. Mable's body gave a little twitch. the monitor was flat lining, giving off a high-pitched continuous whine.

Mable's former home looked different, as if she had adjusted the furniture and straightened the curtains before leaving. It had an empty look. It was clear to me Mable was no longer there.

Ralph took a deep breath. The orange light had slipped into the woods and a dark gray softness was taking its place and surrounding him.

He pulled his seat belt over his chest and put it in the latch, the "click" indicating the task was complete.

"So," he said aloud, "My shadow's getting longer. What's the best use of the time I have left?"

Ralph put the key in the ignition and sat still a few more moments as he stared into the darkness, as if expecting to see something, perhaps an answer to his question.

He turned the ignition key. The engine responded, ending its nap, and began to hum, full of life, ready to transport him wherever he chose to go.

He smiled. He had lots of choices and a little time. He knew he would use some of that time to have tea with Mable. The headlights parted the darkness as Ralph started down the road, continuing his journey. Ralph began to smile as he considered his options. He knew every moment was new, nothing ever being the same.

Ralph reached into the back seat and grabbed a hat.

"I think I'll wear this, my explorer's hat."

Ralph smiled and headed for the land of new adventures.

Changing Perceptions

The mood came again—
A gray cloud-descending—
Choking out positive memories.
A tape of discounts—
And put-downs—and criticism—
Starting to play again—
And, in the pain evoked
By the shrillness—
She hurt herself—to
Quiet the voices
And numb the pain.
The unhealthy alliance
To trade for peace.
The cost—a tiny share of life—
Accumulating.
In confusion—seeing
No options—anything—
To stop the tape-
And she was kicking in her speakers—
Damaging a part of herself—
And the tape played on.
The angel descended—in
A form unexpected—

Revealed only by a shadow
Of butterfly wings
Appearing briefly at twilight—
Whispering to her—with
Gentleness, and compassion—
To change the tape—
To change the tape—
Offering help.

All the tapes in
Her possession had the same
Theme of cruel not-enoughness.
Change the tape—
We'll make a new one—
Recognizing your gifts—
Recognizing your beauty—
Recognizing your enoughness—
Welcomed and wanted
In the world—
Making a new tape.
And as she listened
It sounded strange—
And it took a while for
Her to open her eyes
And see her intense
Beauty—And—as
She opened herself to
Herself,
The healing light burst forth—and
Pulsating through her—

Altering her vision

Of herself.

Oh—the old tapes

Still play,

But she now smiles—

Puts her hand on

A star—and changes

The tape—

And appreciates the

Speakers she

Used to damage—

A gift to herself.

Become the Music

Edwina was tired of being dependent. She had always been a feisty, self-sufficient New Englander, standing up for human rights, the environment, and free speech. She liked to quote "I may disagree with your perception, but I will fight for your right to say it!" Her quick wit led her to make exaggerated and distorted comments about her perceptions, but often her humor was not understood and she was sometimes thought of as a woman that made strange and unrelated remarks during a conversation.

It started when she was ill for an extended period of time. She had, out of necessity, learned to let people assist her in tasks she had been able to do herself. After a period of about a year, she slowly started to get her strength back. She had become cautious about what she was able to do and now would be careful about pushing herself. The less she did the more frustrated she became. Then, at the grocery store, she couldn't lift her bag of groceries.

"Enough of this," she mumbled. She started to read articles on health and fitness. She started doing yoga and Tai Chi. Her diet had always been good, so she only made a few adjustments there. Then she met Jack at the yoga studio. Jack was half her age, very friendly, and a fitness trainer. She asked why he did yoga, and his reasons were similar to hers. In their conversation, Jack told her about the studies that were being done with older people and the benefits of weight training.

Edwina told herself she had bought into the myths of ageism, and decided to fight. Edwina started seeing Jack three times a week, doing resistance training. She got stronger and stronger. The people in the gym were very supportive, giving her hints and encouraging her process.

It was three years to the day when Edwina entered the body builders' contest. Her body was firm and fit. She hung the honorable mention from the contest on the wall. She could now carry her own groceries without effort.

She smiled, "OK–what's next?"

"I wonder—I wonder—if I could become a belly dancer? So I'm old! So what! Look at all my peers. Hanging around, waiting to die!"

Edwina decided to giver herself a 69th birthday present of belly dancing lessons. She was in amazingly good physical shape. Since yoga, Tai Chi, and weight training, her body shape had changed. Her balance had returned. Her flexibility was excellent, and she felt strong and healthy.

She was not surprised when she showed up for her first class at the Y that she was at least twice the age of the oldest members of the class, but she was surprised noting the level of fitness of the rest of the group. Almost half the class seemed very out of shape and somewhat inflexible.

She could feel the music flow through her body. The moves seemed to come so naturally to her, she was surprised to see some of the people having difficulty keeping the beat or getting into the postures suggested by the teacher.

She continued her lessons for the entire year. The faces changed in the classes except for a small core group. Occasionally the group would meet at each others' homes to practice their dancing. Their teacher encouraged them to join her at the Cafe Lebanon where she danced on Saturday nights, but no one had taken up her offer.

Barbara, a tall slender woman who seemed like her every movement was a dance, suggested they all go the club and celebrate Edwina's 70th birthday there. At the class before the planned outing, Edwina's teacher, Swanna, presented her with a gift—a special set of clothing made specially to accent the movements of the dance. The class urged her to put on the outfit for the class. After a little urging, Edwina put on the costume. When Edwina came out of the dressing room, there was a genuine murmur of admiration from the other women. Her body appeared to be that of a woman 30 years younger than her chronological age. She felt free among the women, and danced that night as never before. It seemed some kind of resistance boundary had been broken.

The night of the party, Edwina dressed in her outfit and covered it with a dress she could easily slip off if she chose. There was a live band at the club. The music was more infectious than any they heard on the tapes. Swanna was introduced at the middle of dinner, and among a lot of fanfare, Swanna moved out into the dancing arena and danced—slow, fast, with a variety of movements, now familiar to the group, but never put together as she did in this setting. The music and her dancing were mesmerizing and beautiful.

At one point, Swanna invited people to join her in the dancing. Some people from the audience got up and started dancing, mostly women. There were members of the family of the owner who danced with ease. Edwina's group just watched at first—then, urged on by Swanna, came to the floor and danced.

There was an intermission, and people were being served dessert when Swanna came to the table. She asked Edwina and Barbara to come with her. Swanna led them to a small dressing room in the back, then turned. "I want you both to dance with me when intermission is over. Would you join me?"

Barbara and Edwina looked at each other. Then Edwina started unbuttoning her dress. "Why the hell not! I'm old enough to do anything I want!"

Both Swanna and Barbara grinned, seeing the costume under her dress. "Barbara?" questioned Swanna. Barbara grinned. "How can I say no if Edwina says yes?" Her head tilted as she shrugged her shoulders.

"We'll take turns leading, like we do in class. The drummer is excellent. He will follow your lead, and the rest of the players will follow him. Just let yourself feel the music—then become the music. Don't think, just do."

Swanna offered a costume to Barbara as Edwina slipped off her dress. Swanna changed her costume, very different than the one she had on before intermission.

"When we dance in," instructed Swanna, "Stay a little behind me and dance around me, as if you're my handmaidens. They expect a little razzle dazzle from me, and I will do some things with these veils in the beginning. When I discard the veils, we will dance as we did in class, alone and with each other. Just let it happen. When you lead, let yourself go!"

Edwina could feel her heart pounding as musicians started to play again.

"Let's give a warm greeting to Swanna and her friends, Edwina and Barbara!"

Swanna was right. The music seemed to move her body for her. Barbara and Edwina followed out Swanna, warming up with moves that seemed seamless supporting Swanna's dance with the veils. Swanna, in a flourish, discarded the scarves amidst a thunderous roar of applause. The three women danced facing each other in a circle, then Swanna moved, changing her dance. The drumming followed, but it appeared she was following the drum. Barbara took the lead, her eyes almost closed, flowing and rolling in a way Edwina had never seen her dance before. Then it happened. Edwina felt the music flow through her. She was taking the lead. "Become the music," she could hear Swanna whisper. She felt a sense of aliveness pulsate through her. She knew she was leading the drummer, and he <u>was</u> flawless. Everything she had ever been taught came to her in a soft even flow. She was one with the music—almost in a trance. Then she focused her look. Both Swanna and Barbara were smiling—and she left the lead position. She was startled to hear the thunderous applause, and the drummer was nodding his head, smiling warmly.

Swanna invited the audience to join them, and again people got up and joined the dance. Somehow, through the dance, the women were communicating with each other. Edwina felt a kinship that was new to her, and no longer wondered about how this dance was used by women in other parts of the world. She smiled, and thought, "Happy birthday, Edwina. That was a special gift you gave yourself!"

Options

Even though I drive trucks for a living, I have always wanted to be an opera singer and I have a good voice. I would sing at weddings and parties, but it didn't seem like enough.

Then Fran, my wife, gave me a quality sound unit and a group of opera tapes that were made so a part of the piece would be missing one of the voice parts. On the other side of the tape was the complete piece.

It was made so I could listen to the part I was to sing, then, by playing the other side, I could sing the part with full accompaniment.

The sound unit was battery operated, so I could take it in my truck and listen and sing on my trips.

I can now claim to have sung with some of the greatest opera stars in the world.

When I retired as a trucker, the men from my union chipped in and gave me a trip to Italy, and included guided tours of opera houses and meeting the stars.

There was even one evening that I was permitted to be part of a performance with a live audience. It was intoxicating!

I was encouraged by this troupe to continue singing. They had local workshops so my wife and I stayed in Italy for year and I sang with the teaching troupe. We performed 4 different operas over the year.

Now we are back home. I am doing some writing now. I have also joined a local performance group and sing and act all during the year and in summer stock.

In my writing, I am encouraging people to pursue their dream, and not wait until they retire.

It never dawned on me to take singing lessons and to sing in my spare time when I was working. It wasn't until my wife bought me those tapes that I realized I could do more and by then I was already old by some standards.

It is a wonderful feeling to pursue a dream. I hope I can convey that in my writing, and encourage others not to be discouraged from doing what they really want as early in life as possible.

You want to dance? Dance! So you're 40 and always wanted to do ballet! We both know you probably won't be with the New York City Ballet, but you <u>can</u> dance—and learn, and perform.

You want to paint? Paint! There are people out there that know how to help you get to your inner self—without crippling criticism—helping you express that inner voice, or music, or creating experience, helping you get it out.

Sure—you'll be scared, and worried it's not good enough, and stuff like that, and that's not the point. The point is to get it out. The more you get it out, the easier it gets. Be gentle with yourself. You're a beginner. Make mistakes! Take pleasure in its coming out, not its perfection.

You've got to get it out. It will be rusty, and come in spurts, and be erratic—maybe. Get it out!

It is healing and adds spices to the bland meal of life without it. If it is in you, getting it out will improve the quality of your life.

Watch out for the wet blankets—usually those who are jealous of you having too much fun or only know how to criticize and not know how to encourage.

More than likely, they may include members of your own family.

So find some neat people who know how to support your dream.

Give me a call if you like. It excites me to talk to people who are just tender sprouts beginning to grow in their creativity.

Call me a gardener at heart.

Melody and her Garden

Melody knelt in her garden. Her fluffy white hair drooped over her eyes as she dug holes to plant the tulip bulbs. She sat up, and, as she brushed the hair from her face, smiled. It was that kind of smile that made anyone with her feel safe and at ease.

She was remembering. She was remembering when she and John first planted tulips in this very garden over 40 years ago. He had been a city boy, and gardening was new to him. He seemed awkward and hesitant about what to do, but his excitement and enthusiasm overcame any reservations he had. She knew, knowing him as she did, that the excitement was about being with her and not about making holes in the ground.

Even then she had crooked duck-turned ankles. After they were married, and he learned she was self-conscious about them, he would massage her feet and kiss those ankles in loving adoration, and she learned to love them too.

He had died ten years ago. The heart attack was sudden, unexpected, and fatal. It took her two wintry years before she got tired of feeling numb, and one spring evening she picked a bunch of daffodils and put them on her table that she had filled with lit candles. She spent the night writing to John, telling him about her pain and loneliness, and by dawn, she sensed his talking back to her, reminding her of the many pleasures they had together.

As the sun rose that day, she started to see the beauty around her again, and John's favorite bush or flowers started to trigger warm feelings and pleasant memories, replacing the hollow emptiness that she had been feeling inside her. She discovered that digging in her garden triggered nice memories of being with him, as if he were there whispering to her.

Winter was the most difficult time for her. She had a lot of indoor plants, but they didn't have the same effect as digging outdoors in the garden. That was, until last year. Last year she experienced John's presence when she decided to bake some bread, something she hadn't done for a long time.

The smell of the yeast and fresh dough, the aroma of baking bread, the sight of butter melting on the fresh cut warm bread opened another door for her.

She had forgotten, until then, how delighted he was when, during that first year he met her, she had served him bread she had just made. He had been very impressed. He never had homemade bread before, let alone bread warm from the oven! He praised her and thanked her so much she felt embarrassed, since baking bread was such a simple thing for her to do.

As she got to know John better, though, she realized it was the simple, common, everyday things that he appreciated so much. His work life was full of complexities, and he always seemed excited to come home.

When the Lilies of the Valley came up, she would remember him coming into the house with a handful of them, and, with a big grin, would put them in water. He would sit and stare at them, as if expecting them to ring. He reminded her of a little boy, excited about bringing his mother a bouquet of dandelions.

Each year when the flowers on the bushes and trees came out, he always seemed amazed the blossoms came out before the leaves. Each year he greeted the flowers with the same sense of surprise and awe, as if experiencing the event for the first time.

Lately, there were times she thought she could feel his breath on her neck, and just before spring, during a night when her back felt cold and in pain, she felt as if he was snuggling with her, and the cold and the pain went away.

As summer passed, the pain in her body got more intense and lasted longer. She started to feel John's presence more often, attempting to comfort her.

It was when the trees started to change color that she saw him. He held out his arms to her, and she went to him and put her head on his shoulder as he held her. She looked back at that part of her who had so faithfully housed her, now cold and stiff without her presence, turned back to John and kissed him gently. Holding his hands, she stepped back slightly and looked into his warm and loving eyes. They both turned and walked through the door to the sunlight garden full of flowers, hand in hand, together.

The Hero

The daily paper had a small article about the event buried somewhere in the middle, but the weekly paper, The Town Crier, thought it worthy of a front page story.

"DOG SAVES FAMILY!" the headline read. The story described how the family dog woke up its owners, who in turn woke up their guest, and how the family members were able to extinguish the source of the smoke that was filling the house. The smoke detectors went off long after the dog had awakened its owners, averting a possible tragedy.

An event with almost no damage and no injuries or deaths wasn't considered very newsworthy, but The Town Crier made it a human interest story focusing on the value of dogs and with this loyal dog, always alert and on watch, the hero of the story. A picture of King looked back at David as he read the story. It was true, sort of. When the reporter arrived with the fire truck, David had simply said the dog woke him up and he noticed the smoke.

He looked at the picture again and smiled. He hadn't wanted a dog, but Susan did. She said said a dog would alert them to intruders or help in the event of an emergency, just as the story in front of him described.

David smiled again as he thought of what happened that night.

A friend he hadn't seen in over a year was going to be in the area on business, so they agreed that Bill would stay with David and Susan when he came to town. He would arrive on a very late plane and would be renting a car, so they told him where to find the key to the house and to let himself in. King was a big dog, and friendly. When Bill arrived that night, King was sleeping by the door. King stood up as Bill entered the house, sniffed him, and walked into Sue and David's bedroom, as if annoyed he had been awakened. No barking, no growling, nothing but a sniff. Bill knew his way to the guest-room and settled in for the night.

It was later that David was awakened by King. King did not bark, or whine, or nudge him. He didn't pull the blankets off the bed with his mouth.

What he did do was snore. The dog was snoring so loudly it woke David up. The noisy snoring continued, keeping David from going back to sleep, and that is when David noticed the smoke. So it was true that King woke him up.

David looked up from the paper as he felt King rub past him. He rose, went to the cabinet and got King a dog biscuit. That was the least you could do for a Hero!

Romance

D avid looked through the tiny two windows over the sink, watching the yellow VW grow smaller and smaller as it drove down the dirt road, mists of dust chasing it, rows of corn as tall as the car, waving nervously as the car passed.

The early morning sun stabbed the lacy curtains, making them appear like tiny embers, emitting a magical light—matching David's internal glow.

The kettle whistled—startling him—drawing him toward the present moment.

David smiled as he poured water into the sink, smiling at the awakening bubbles swimming across the surface of the water.

H picked up her cup, and rubbed his fingers across the smooth edge, then gently placed it—very slowly—in the water.

He rubbed the cup, now moist with warm soapy water, enjoying the sensation of the smooth surface of the cup on his fingers. With utmost care and gentleness he placed the cup on the bottom of the sink. As he drew his hands slowly out of the soapy water, he enjoyed the pleasurable way the water caressed him, leaving bubbles on his forearms, wrists and hands.

Smiling, he reached for the saucer, and, as if doing a meditation in motion—he moved with extreme slowness—parting the bubbles with the saucer, then moving the disc into the soapy warmth, then wet, caressing the saucer, rubbing any remnants of coffee off—oh—so gently—enjoying the pleasure of the warm smooth china on his fingers.

David continued the process, maintaining a slowness that would have irritated someone anxious to complete the task, but it would be apparent to any observe that David was in a pleasurable meditative state as he performed the task.

He took his own cup and saucer and treated it with the same careful reverence as he did the two plates, the knives, forks and spoons.

He looked at the frying pan and the spatula, and decided to wait until he finished the dishes and utensils he currently caressed until they were tenderly rinsed and carefully, slowly dried.

He placed the cups and saucers in the cupboard with an unnecessary gentleness, placing the paired china and utensils—2 at a time—in their usual place, each with a caress before closing the door or drawer.

Chimen Bird

He was full of excitement! This was the day he had been waiting for for the past five years. It was the day the rare <u>Chimen</u> bird would appear here at its namesake, the Gate of Hope. It now only returns for a few hours to rest, rather than nest for weeks as it had done in the past. Something had changed its migratory pattern, yet it still returns here once a year to its original Asian origin. Ralph felt like the universe was supporting him when, after 5 years of searching, he discovered the offering of a spirituality workshop being held at this sacred spot at a house on a hill over looking the twin mountain opening—"the Gate of Hope". The protected bay within had saved many fishermen from unexpected storms, and the screeching of the birds were considered sacred sounds and prayers by the locals.

It was the third day of the retreat. Ralph felt a little fuzzy, waking up just before dawn. He hurried to the candlelit kitchen and grabbed a ceramic cup, its C-shaped handle balanced evenly in the middle of the cup.

It seemed everyone was already gathered for the "mindful eating" exercise on the dining porch, so he quickly thrust his cup under the coffee urn, pulled the handle, and looked toward the porch. It was then he felt it, warm burning sensations on his bared feet. He wondered if he had stepped in a nest of biting insects when he became aware his coffee cup was upside down and the coffee was splattering on the floor and splashing onto his feet.

A hand reached in front of him before the connection registered and pushed the handle on the coffee urn to an "off" position. The petit Asian woman slowly shook her head as she looked at him, her long black hair moving in waves down her back.

Ralph hurried to the eating area. The "mindful eating" exercise had already begun, but he was in time to hear the instructor say to take the raisin and take a deep breath in, detecting any subtle aromas. Ralph put a raisin under one of his nostrils, and closed off the other nostril so he wouldn't be distracted by other scents. He took a deep breath in and was surprised to feel the raisin fly up his nose—a rocket trying to reach his brain . . . .

The tiny Asian woman was looking up his nose with a flashlight—shaking her head. The chopsticks went into his nose easily enough, and her skill with them made the raisin removal almost painless. Ralph rejoiced at his good luck to have someone so skilled with chopsticks to be so near at hand!

He got to the group assembly late. The instructions were already given, and it was now a time of silence. As he walked in, the group stood up and started to disperse. He decided to just follow someone that had been in his smaller group, so he chose Anna. She had seemed very friendly and he had been somewhat attracted to her.

He followed her down the hall—then up a flight of stairs, and then down a long corridor. He didn't want to intrude on her private space, so Ralph kept a respectful distance behind her.

She turned a corner and Ralph followed. As he turned the corner, he saw a flashing light, then darkness.

As he awoke, his nose felt sore. The two-by-four Anna hit him with had made a slash across hi forehead.

Later he apologized to Anna. He didn't know she was in her 7th year of therapy recovering from a stalking incident.

Someone shouted "The birds are coming!" Hurrying to the terrace, he checked his camera. Film OK. Batteries new. The light was just right. He pointed the camera up at the low-flying birds overhead.

His dream was about to be realized.

"Splat!" The white fluid covered the lens completely.

Ralph stood quietly for a moment—then smiled broadly.

He had <u>more</u> than a <u>picture!</u>—he had an authentic dropping from the Sacred Chimen bird!

Surprise!

The moon peeked around the cloud, lighting the curved pathway among the trees, enough light to make out the figure on the park bench.

It was odd-ball Earl—the eccentric wealthy owner of the penthouse next to the park.

He was wearing his striped beanie with the propeller on the top, a sweatshirt with a snake on the front and letters that read, "Don't Tread on Me" underneath.

He had a computer on his lap and was typing furiously. He didn't see the three tuffs coming down the path from his left. You could tell they were looking for trouble by their swagger and dress. They were wearing their warrior colors of red and yellow striped shirts.

I didn't know what to do! I didn't think I could reach him in time to warn him—and that beanie hat! That was enough to invite trouble in the park at night.

They stopped at the bench and started talking and laughing. Earl got up after calmly closing his computer and putting it on the bench.

Two of the men were facing him as the third moved to his side. One of the men in front of him said something and Earl laughed.

The man seemed annoyed at the response, reached up and knocked Earl's beanie off his head.

I could see Earl's face change to anger, even from the distance from which I watched, hidden in the trees.

The same man reached out to grab Earl, while the man at his side drew out a knife, the blade sparkling in the moonlight.

Oh—Earl—such innocence! Such stupidity—in the park at night—with your beanie hat on.

There was a blur of movement. I couldn't believe it! Earl moved so quickly I didn't see it. The knife had moved, but slashed at the man who had knocked Earl's hat off!

Earl's foot pushed the knife holder's arm, moving the shiny blade deep into the man who had threatened him.

Another blur. The other man who had originally faced Earl was on the ground, moaning and holding his nose, blood running down his face, then became quiet.

The third man looked at Earl a moment, turned and ran.

Earl bent over, picked up his hat and placed it back on his head.

He pulled out a cell phone, made a call, I guess to the police, put the phone back into his pocket, sat on the bench and opened his computer. He propped his feet up on the two men lying in front of the bench and began typing furiously.

I guess odd-ball Earl doesn't like to be interrupted when he is working on a task!

John's Gift Box

ohn smiled. He finished wrapping the little white cardboard box in shiny silver paper. John then wrapped a ribbon around the small square package, but had difficulty with his fat, seven year old fingers manipulating the ribbon.

John frowned, making his crew-cut hair change shape—then removed the ribbon. He picked up the sliver bow, pulled of the adhesive, and put it on the box. "It doesn't need any ribbon," he mumbled to himself.

Later that evening, John's father came home with Ernie, and occasional friend. John didn't like Ernie. He seemed mean, and didn't understand why his father liked him around.

John's mother and father and Ernie were sitting around the kitchen table when John brought the package into the room and placed it in front of his father.

"And what's this?" asked John's father.

"A Father's Day present, just for you."

John's father opened the little package, then removed the lid and looked in the box. "It seems empty," said John's father, with caution.

John's face was beaming. "No! It's full! I filled it with a lot of happy thoughts, and little pieces of time that felt nice and quiet. You said to Mummy you didn't have much quiet time, and sometimes you felt sad about losing your job. So I collected some quiet time and happy thoughts for you."

John's mother was smiling, as was John's dad.

Ernie snorted. "You can't collect happiness or time and put it in a <u>box</u>."

John's dad gave Ernie a dirty look. "My son can," John's dad said quietly to Ernie. "Maybe you can't, Ernie, but my son can."

John looked at Ernie. "It makes me sad you can't put nice things in a box, Mr. Ernie. Maybe I can collect something for you that could help you."

Dog and Friend

He didn't trust Dog. It was a big dog, 110 pounds, and had been abused before they adopted it. She loved the dog. A connection had been made between them. The occasional strange behaviors were to be expected, She said.

Dog had an unusually anxious night. Dog had chewed and licked his paws noisily, keeping He awake, and He woke up grouchy. She left for work. He didn't want the dog to chew up clothing or shoes left in the bedroom, so he attempted to coax Dog out to another room. Dog was behaving strangely again. Dog had walked to the corner of the bedroom at the far end of the room, head toward the corner and just stood there. Dog did not respond to He's calls. Annoyed, He went to the corner to take Dog out by the collar.

It was twilight when She returned home. Dog greeted her playfully at the door, jumping and spinning, running playfully back and forth. "Show me your bone," She said. And Dog brought what she thought was a rawhide bone and Dog ran up and down the hall with it. Then, with his front legs bent in a prayer position, his hind legs high, Dog presented his offering to She. The scene was so adorable, She thought, and put her glasses on so she could enjoy the moment in sharp focus.

It wasn't a piece of rawhide, but a forearm and hand that was between his paws. She quickly went through the house, and found He in the corner of the bedroom—with his throat ripped out. The right arm had been chewed off at the elbow. She looked at the bloody scene in horror and shock, standing there for a long time, looking, as her eyes became glassy.

Dog nuzzled against her leg, and trotted toward the door, beckoning her with his head. "Yes," She said. "I'll take you out." On the word "out", Dog's head tilted, and he became excited. "Naughty dog," She said, gently chastising. "Look at the mess you made! Well, I'll clean it up after our walk." She took Dog for a walk, her friend and protector, bonded.

Fluffy Feathers

I never thought much about Roberta until I noticed, in a small exhibit at the Museum of Science, an interesting fluff of feather, recalling the day we discovered the remnants of a bird as we were walking the trail behind her home near the lake. It was difficult to tell from the ragged piece of body left, still covered with light fluffy feathers rimmed by strong, smooth and highly textured quills of brown-white beauty, what kind of bird it had been. There were loose, curled whisps of fluff scattered in the area, along with several of the firm and straight feathers, the light bouncing on their shiny lined surface, the remnants of a beautiful and breathing creature, scattered.

Roberta looked sad. Then taking a silk-smooth scarf from her purse, she gathered the strong pointed and stiff quills and the curly puffs of whispy fluffs and carefully wrapped the scarf around her treasure.

When we returned to her house, she seemed like she was in a trance and walked directly to her studio, placed a goose-bumpy canvas on her easel, prepared some acrylic paints on her palette, and quickly changed the texture of the canvas to a streaky display of color, some smoothed and some creviced. Quickly a shape emerged—an image of what might have been the unhappy bird whose feathers we had found.

Then Roberta carefully pulled open her scarf. After studying the pile of collected softness, she chose several of the fluff feathers and stuck them into the paint. She chose only one of the large firm feathers and also pushed it into the tiny mounds of color. After a little arranging, the bird seemed to be lifting out of the canvas—almost alive—its softness framed against the dark roughness of shadowy background.

She stood up straight, brushed several thick round strands of black hair away from her sticky forehead, and stared.

I followed her gaze. We both looked at the picture. A delicate, feathery puff, soft with a grayish cluster, moved very gently in the breeze.

She mumbled dreamily, "I think I might have lived at that time—I remember—soft feathers—I remember—being free."

She looked at me, her eyes still glazed. "I've been a bird, you see—I've been many forms. And now, I recreate—rebuild—and the spirit is reborn in my painting and another life form is added to the universe—in a different place, at a different time."

The lines around her eyes seemed to become less deep as she spoke, and suddenly a shimmering yellow light surrounded her—vibrating dark and light. Then the light intensified and the texture of her body became transparent—moving, the whirling and swirling in a funnel shape. With a slurping sound, the light was absorbed into the painting!

I stared as the painting stirred. The bird emerged and flew off the easel, through the door and out into the open courtyard. It landed on a rugged prickly brown bush, as if waiting for me to follow.

As I got close, it flew again, leading me back to the place we first discovered the feathers.

There was a bright flash of jagged light. I felt as if the light was slicing through the tiny pores of my skin, and everything went black.

I opened my eyes. I was lying on the ground on the path. I could feel the rough, stiff grass dig into my body.

Roberta was wiping my forehead with a rough wet cloth, cool to the touch. I sat up quickly and looked around.

There were only a few feathers on the ground. I looked at Roberta. Her eyes were no longer glazed.

She said, "I was so worried. You must have fallen and hit your head. Are you ok?"

I got up, feeling the ground rock back and forth under me.

We walked back to the house in silence.

I left for home shortly after we returned to her house. I haven't seen Roberta since that unusual day.

The Tye-Dyed Cloth

Astra put the tie-died cloth back in place. It had come loose from its back-lit frame. She turned on the light, tilted her head to the left, and smiled. It had a stained glass appearance with intensely-warm colors, inviting the viewer to sit and relax and talk of old times. It had been 32 years since Astra had made the piece, and it still gave her the sense of glowing satisfaction it had given her when she first made it.

She continued smiling, turned and went to the kitchen. Dennis was sitting on a stool drinking a cup of tea and reading a health newsletter, a second cup next to him on the counter. "I made you cup of tea," he said without looking up. "Thanks," she mumbled. "Why does he do this—leave the teabag in too long!" she thought to herself. "He never gets anything right!" She was no longer smiling—only looking at him with stony eyes.

"What's wrong?" he asked, looking up. He had sensed a change in mood.

"Nothing! Any messages for me?"

"Yes—that Mrs. Brightly wants you to come over and exorcise some kind of ghost." His smile irritated her. He never was able to see her beauty, her magical self, her giftedness.

She could feel herself simmering on the inside.

"Well, let's go," he said abruptly, putting down the newsletter. "You wanted to see the new exhibit."

"Yes," she said, "Just a minute." She went to a side room of glass, filled with a variety of plants. As if talking with them without words, she walked around the room, touching each plant as she walked by, smiled, and, as if energized, walked briskly toward the door.

At the museum, they agreed on a place to meet after 1 hour. Astra walked slowly, examining all the details of a picture. Up close, from a distance, then at a medium distance, she would stand in front of a picture, and seemed to move into it.

Dennis buzzed the exhibit. He'd look briefly at each picture until he saw all the new offering. He then went through the rest of the museum in the same manner, looked at his watch, and smiled. He still had a half hour to have a coffee in the museum café.

Astra was entranced by a picture of a small pond, water trickling down random rocks, surrounded by a dense growth of wide leafy vines.

She could feel the vines coming out the picture, greeting her, appreciating her connecting. She sensed something behind her. She recognized the vibration—that hateful vibration from Dennis.

She closed her eyes and concentrated. Instead of feeling neutral, all she could feel was hate—a venomous hate with an intensity she never felt before.

She opened her eyes and turned to him. He smiled warmly at her. "Ready?" he asked.

"In a minute. Dennis, come over here and stand in front of this picture."

Dennis shrugged, and moved, used to unusual requests from Astra.

"Now close your eyes," she said, almost whispering.

She looked around. They were alone in the gallery.

Her eyes glazed and she stared again at the picture. The vines again grew out and wrapped around him without touching him.

Dennis continued to stand with his eyes closed as instructed.

Astra nodded her head.

The vines tightened around Dennis—moving very quietly. "Hey! What's going on?" bellowed Dennis.—Then, he was gone.

She watched as the vines in the picture dragged Dennis to the pond and pushing and pulling him under the water. There was some splashing, and then there was no movement in the water. The vines went back to their original setting.

Astra smiled.

She got up and drove home alone, the grin remaining on her face.

She smiled and felt warm as she walked past the lighted tye-dye cloth, put on the kettle for tea, and sat in her plant room, waiting for the kettle to signal the water was ready.